About Natalia Ginzburg and *The Dry Heart*

"Ginzburg never raises her voice, never strains for effect, never judges her creations. Like Chekhov, she knows how to stand back and let her characters expose their own lives, their frailties and strengths, their illusions and private griefs. The result is nearly translucent writing—writing so clear, so direct, so seemingly simple that it gives the reader the magical sense of apprehending the world for the first time."
—Michiko Kakutani, *The New York Times*

"Her prose style is deceptively simple and very complex. Its effect on the reader is both calming and thrilling—that's not so easy to do."
—Deborah Levy

"Her sentences have great precision and clarity, and I learn a lot when I read her."
—Zadie Smith

"I'm always drawn to short novels that pack a punch—Fleur Jaeggy's *Sweet Days of Discipline* (101 pages), Willem Frederick Hermans's *An Untouched House* (88 pages), and José Revueltas's *The Hole* (79 pages) are all the more powerful for how brief they are. It's less about finding the time to read Natalia Ginzburg's *The Dry Heart*, an 83-page novel about an Italian woman who shoots and kills her husband on page one, than it is preparing yourself for it."
—Gabe Habash, *Publishers Weekly Best Summer Reads 2019*

"If Ferrante is a friend, Ginzburg is a mentor."
 —*The Guardian*

"Ginzburg gives us a new template for the female voice and an idea of what it might sound like. This voice emerges from her preoccupations and themes, whose specificity and universality she considers with a gravitas and authority that seem both familiar and entirely original."
 —Rachel Cusk

"Filled with shimmering, risky, darting observation."
 —Colm Tóibín

"The raw beauty of Ginzburg's prose compels our gaze. First we look inward, with the shock of recognition inspired by all great writing, and then, inevitably, out at the shared world she evokes with such uncompromising clarity."
 —Hilma Wolitzer

"There is no one quite like Ginzburg for telling it like it is."
 —Phillip Lopate

"Ginzburg's beautiful words have such solidity and simplicity. I read her with joy and amazement."
 —Tessa Hadley

"Her simplicity is an achievement, hard-won and remarkable, and the more welcome in a literary world where the cloak of omniscience is all too readily donned."
 —William Weaver, *The New York Times*

The Dry Heart

By NATALIA GINZBURG
FROM NEW DIRECTIONS

The Dry Heart
Happiness, as Such

Natalia Ginzburg
The Dry Heart

Translated from the Italian
by Frances Frenaye

A NEW DIRECTIONS PAPERBOOK

Originally published in Italian as *È stato così*. Published by arrangement with the Estate of Natalia Ginzburg and Giulio Einaudi Editore SpA

Manufactured in the United States of America

First published as a New Directions Paperbook (NDP1448) in 2019

Library of Congress Cataloging-in-Publication Data
Names: Ginzburg, Natalia, author. | Frenaye, Frances, 1908–1996, translator.
Title: The dry heart / Natalia Ginzburg ; translated by Frances Frenaye.
Other titles: È stato cosi. English
Description: New York : New Directions, 2019. | "A New Directions Book." | English translation originally published by The Hogarth Press Ltd. in 1952.
Identifiers: LCCN 2019004340 | ISBN 9780811228787 (alk. paper)
Subjects: LCSH: Marriage—Fiction. | Parricide—Fiction. | Murder—Fiction.
Classification: LCC PQ4817.I5 E213 2019 | DDC 853/.912—dc23
LC record available at https://lccn.loc.gov/2019004340

10 9 8 7 6 5 4

New Directions Books are published for James Laughlin
by New Directions Publishing Corporation
80 Eighth Avenue, New York 10011

The Dry Heart

"TELL ME THE TRUTH," I SAID.

"What truth?" he echoed. He was making a rapid sketch in his notebook and now he showed me what it was: a long, long train with a big cloud of black smoke swirling over it and himself leaning out of a window to wave a handkerchief.

I shot him between the eyes.

He had asked me to give him something hot in a thermos bottle to take with him on his trip. I went into the kitchen, made some tea, put milk and sugar in it, screwed the top on tight, and went back into his study. It was then that he showed me the sketch, and I took the revolver out of his desk drawer and shot him between the eyes. But for a long time already I had known that sooner or later I should do something of the sort.

I put on my raincoat and gloves and went out. I drank a cup of coffee at the counter of a café and walked haphazardly about the city. It was a chilly day and a damp wind was blowing. I sat down on a bench in the park, took off my gloves and looked at my hands. Then I slipped off my wedding ring and put it in my pocket.

We had been husband and wife for four years. He had threatened often enough to leave me, but then our baby died and we stayed together. Another child, he said, would be my salvation.

For this reason we made love frequently toward the end, but nothing came of it.

I found him packing his bags and asked him where he was going. He said he was going to Rome to settle something with a lawyer and suggested I visit my parents so as not to be alone in the house while he was away. He didn't know when he'd be back, in two weeks or a month, he couldn't really say. It occurred to me that he might never come back at all. Meanwhile I packed my bags too. He told me to take some books with me to while away the time and I pulled *Vanity Fair* and two volumes of Galsworthy out of the bookcase and put them in one of my bags.

"Tell me the truth, Alberto," I said.

"What truth?" he echoed.

"You are going away together."

"Who are going away together? You let your imagination run riot. You eat your heart out thinking up terrible things. That way you've no peace of mind and neither has anyone else.... Take the bus that gets to Maona at two o'clock," he said.

"Yes," I answered.

He looked at the sky and remarked: "Better wear your raincoat and galoshes."

"I'd rather know the truth, whatever it may be," I said, and he laughed and misquoted:

> She seeketh Truth, which is so dear
> As knoweth he who life for her refuses.*

I sat on the bench for I don't know how long. The park was deserted, the benches were drenched with dew, and the ground

---

* "He seeketh Liberty ..." (Dante, *Purgatory*, I, 71).

4

was strewn with wet leaves. I began to think about what I should do next. After a while I said to myself, "I should go to the police and try to tell them how it all came about." But that would be no easy matter. I should have to go back to the day when we first met, at the house of Dr. Gaudenzi. He was playing a piano duet with the doctor's wife and singing dialect songs. He looked at me hard and made a pencil sketch of me in his notebook. I said it was a good likeness, but he said it wasn't and tore it up.

"He can never draw the women that really attract him," said Dr. Gaudenzi.

They gave me a cigarette and laughed to see how it made my eyes water. Alberto took me back to my boardinghouse and asked if he could come the next day to bring me a French novel which he had mentioned in the course of the evening.

The next day he came. We went out for a walk and ended up in a café. His eyes were gay and sparkling and I began to think he was in love with me. I was very happy, because no man had ever fallen in love with me before, and I could have sat with him in the café indefinitely. That evening we went to the theatre and I wore my best dress, a crimson velvet given me by my cousin Francesca.

Francesca was at the theatre, too, a few rows behind us, and waved to me. The next day, when I went to lunch at the house of my aunt and uncle, she asked me:

"Who was that old man?"

"What old man?"

"The old man at the theatre."

I told her he was someone who was interested in me but that I didn't care for him one way or the other. When he came back to the boardinghouse to see me I looked him over and he didn't seem so very old to me. Francesca called everyone old. I didn't really like him, and the only reason I was pleased to have him come and call on me was that he looked at me with such gay and sparkling eyes. Every woman is pleased when a man looks at her like that. I thought he must be very much in love. "Poor fellow!" I thought to myself, and I imagined his asking me to marry him and the words he would say. I would answer no, and he would ask if we could still be friends. He would keep on taking me to the theatre and one evening he would introduce me to a friend, much younger than himself, who would fall in love with me, and this was the man I should marry. We should have a lot of children and Alberto would come to call. Every Christmas he would bring us a big fruitcake and there would be a touch of melancholy in his enjoyment of our happiness.

Lying dreamily on the bed in my boardinghouse room, I imagined how wonderful it would be to be married and have a house of my own. In my imagination I saw exactly how I should arrange my house, with dozens of stylish gadgets and potted plants, and I visualized myself sitting in an armchair over a basket of embroidery. The face of the man I married was constantly changing, but he had always the same voice, which I could hear repeating over and over again the same ironical and tender phrases. The boardinghouse was gloomy, with dark hangings and upholstery, and in the room next to mine a colonel's widow knocked on the wall with a hairbrush every time I opened the window or moved a chair. I had to get up early in order to arrive on time at the school where I was a teacher. I dressed in a hurry and ate a roll and an egg which I boiled over a tiny alcohol stove. The colonel's widow knocked furiously on the wall while I moved about the room looking for my clothes, and in the bathroom the landlady's hysterical daughter screeched like a peacock while they gave her a warm shower which was supposed to calm her down. I rushed out on to the street and while I waited in the cold and lonely dawn for the tram, I made up all sorts of stories to keep myself warm, so that sometimes I arrived at school with a wild and absent look on my face that must have been positively funny.

A girl likes to think that a man may be in love with her, and even if she doesn't love him in return it's almost as if she did. She is prettier than usual and her eyes shine; she walks at a faster pace and the tone of her voice is softer and sweeter. Before I knew Alberto I used to feel so dull and unattractive that I was sure I should always be alone, but after I got the impression that he was in love with me I began to think that if I could please him then I might please someone else, too, perhaps the man who spoke to me in ironical and tender phrases in my imagination. This man had a constantly changing face, but he always had broad shoulders and red, slightly awkward hands and an utterly charming way of teasing me every evening when he came home and found me sitting over my embroidery.

When a girl is very much alone and leads a tiresome and monotonous existence, with worn gloves and very little spending money, she may let her imagination run wild and find herself defenceless before all the errors and pitfalls which imagination has devised to deceive her. I was a weak and unarmed victim of imagination as I read Ovid to eighteen girls huddled in a cold classroom or ate my meals in the dingy boardinghouse dining room, peering out through the yellow windowpanes as I waited for Alberto to take me out walking or to a concert. Every Saturday afternoon I took the bus to Maona, returning on Sunday evening.

My father has been a country doctor at Maona for over twenty years. He is a tall, stout, slightly lame old man who uses a cherrywood cane for walking. In summer he wears a straw hat with a black ribbon around it and in winter a beaver cap and an overcoat with a beaver collar. My mother is a tiny woman with a thick mass of white hair. My father has few calls because he is old and moves about with difficulty. When people are sick they call the doctor from Cavapietra, who has a motorcycle and studied medicine at Naples. My father and mother sit in the kitchen all day long playing chess with the local vet and the tax collector. On Saturdays when I came to Maona I sat down by the kitchen stove and there I sat all day Sunday until it was time to go. I roasted myself there by the stove, stuffed with thick soups and corn meal, and did not so much as open my mouth, while between one game of chess and the next my father told the vet that modern girls have no respect for their parents and do not tell them a word of what they are doing.

I used to tell Alberto about my father and mother and the life I led at Maona before I came to teach in the city. I told him how my father used to rap me over the fingers with his cane and I used to run and cry in the coal cellar. How I used to hide *From Slavegirl to Queen* under my mattress to read at night and how, when my father and the tax collector and the maidservant and I used to walk down the road between the fields and vineyards to the cemetery, I had a violent longing to run away.

Alberto never told me anything about himself, and I fell into the habit of asking him no questions. It had never happened before that anyone should take such an interest in me and attribute so much importance to what I had felt and said in the coal cellar or on the road to the cemetery. When I went for a walk with Alberto or when we sat in a café together I was happy and no longer felt so alone. Alberto told me that he lived with his mother, who was old and ailing. Dr. Gaudenzi's wife informed me that she was a very rich but batty old woman who spent her time smoking cigarettes in an ivory holder and studying Sanskrit, and that she never saw anyone except a Dominican friar who came every evening to read her the Epistles of Saint Paul. On the pretext that she could not get her shoes on without hurting her feet she had not left the house for years, but sat all day long in an armchair, in the care of a young servant girl who cheated her on food bills and maltreated her into the bargain. At first I didn't mind Alberto's unwillingness to talk about himself, but later I was disappointed and asked him a few questions. His face took on an absent and faraway expression and his eyes were veiled with mist like those of a sick bird whenever I inquired about his mother, or his work, or any other part of his life.

He never said that he was in love with me, but he came regularly to see me, bringing me books and chocolates, and wanting to take me out with him. I thought he might be shy and afraid to speak up, and I waited for him to say that he loved me so that I could tell Francesca. Francesca always had so much to tell and I never had anything. Finally, although he still hadn't spoken, I told Francesca all the same. That day he had given me some tan kid gloves and I was sure that he must love me after all. I told her that he was too old for me to marry, although I didn't really know how old he was—forty, perhaps—while I was only twenty-six. Francesca told me to get rid of him, that she didn't like his looks, and that I should throw the gloves back in his face because the snaps at the wrist were long since out of style and made me look like a country bumpkin. She'd always suspected, she said, that this fellow would bring me trouble. Francesca was only twenty at the time, but I respected her common sense and always listened to what she had to say.

But this time I didn't listen. I liked the gloves in spite of the snaps at the wrist and went on wearing them, and I liked Alberto, too, and continued to see him. After twenty-six years life had seemed empty and sad because no man had ever paid any attention to me, much less given me gifts. It was all very easy for Francesca to talk that way, when she had everything she wanted and was always travelling and amusing herself.

Then summer came and I went to Maona. I expected Alberto to write, but he never sent me anything but his signature on a picture postcard of a village on the lakes. I was bored with Maona and the days seemed never to go by. I sat in the kitchen or stretched out on my bed to read. My mother, with her head wrapped in a napkin, peeled tomatoes on the porch and laid them out to dry on a board, for making preserves, while my father sat on the wall of the square in front of our house with the vet and the tax collector, tracing signs in the dust with his cane. The maidservant washed clothes at the fountain in the courtyard and wrung them out with her heavy red arms; flies buzzed over the tomatoes, and my mother wiped her knife on a newspaper and dried her sticky hands. I looked at Alberto's postcard until I knew the contents of the picture by heart: a ray of sun striking a sailing boat on the lake. Why had he sent me nothing but this? Francesca wrote me two letters from Rome, where she had gone with a friend to study at a school of dramatics. First she said that she was engaged to be married and then that it was all off.

I often thought that Alberto might come to Maona to see me. My father would be surprised until I explained that he was a friend of Dr. Gaudenzi. I used to go into the kitchen and carry the garbage pail down to the coal cellar because it had such a bad smell, but the maidservant said that it had no smell at all and carried it back to the kitchen. On the one hand I was afraid to see Alberto appear, because I was ashamed of the garbage pail and of the way my mother looked with a napkin wrapped around her head and her hands sticky with tomatoes; on the other, I waited eagerly for his arrival, and every time the bus came I looked out the window to see if he was on it. I breathed hard and shook all over every time I saw a slight figure in a light raincoat get off, but when I realized that it was not Alberto I went back into my room to read and daydream until dinner. Often I tried to dream again of the man with the broad shoulders and ironical manner, but he drifted farther and farther away until his anonymous and changing face lost all significance.

When I came back to the city I expected that Alberto would turn up soon. He must guess that I had to return for the opening of school. Every evening I powdered and primped and sat waiting; then, when he failed to come, I went to bed. The boardinghouse was gloomy and desolate with its dark flowered hangings and upholstery and the screeching of the landlady's daughter when she refused to get undressed. I had Alberto's address and telephone number, but I didn't dare try to get in touch with him because he had always taken the initiative of telephoning me. Perhaps, I thought, he had not yet come back. One day I called his number from a public telephone booth and his voice answered. But I hung up the receiver without saying a word. Every evening I primped and powdered and waited. I was half ashamed of myself and tried to cover up my air of expectancy by reading a book, but the words made no sense. The nights were still warm, and through the open window I could hear the trams on the boulevards. I imagined him riding in one of them with his light raincoat and leather briefcase, going about one of the mysterious activities which he was never willing to talk about.

This, then, is how I fell in love with him, sitting all powdered and primped in my boardinghouse bedroom while the half-hours and hours went by, accompanied by the screeching of the landlady's daughter, or walking in the city streets, on the alert for his unexpected appearance, and with a quickened pulse every time I saw a slight figure in a light raincoat holding one shoulder a little higher than the other. I began to think constantly of his life, how he managed being in the house with a mother who studied Sanskrit and refused to put on her shoes. I said to myself that if he asked me I would marry him, and then I would know at every hour of the day where he was and what he was doing. Every evening when he came home he would throw his raincoat over a chair in the hall and I would hang it up in the closet. Francesca had not yet come back from Rome, but when she came she would surely ask about Alberto, and when I told her I had not seen him again she would exclaim: "How does that happen, if he was in love with you?" and I would be embarrassed.

I went to the Gaudenzi house one day to see if he was there or if they had news of him. The doctor wasn't at home and his wife was washing the windows. While I watched her polish them she told me that the system was to clean them with a solution of ashes and then to rub them slowly with a wool cloth. Then she came down from the ladder and made me a cup of hot chocolate. But she said not a word about Alberto, so I went away.

Finally one day I met him on the street. I saw him from a distance with his briefcase under his arm and his raincoat open and flapping. I walked behind him for a while as he smoked a cigarette and flicked the ashes away. Then he stopped and turned around in order to stamp out the butt and saw me. He was very pleased and took me to a café. He told me that it was only because he was very busy that he had not come to call, but that he had thought of me often. I looked at him and tried to recognize in this little man with the curly black hair the cause of all my anguish and torment. I felt cold and humiliated and as if something inside me were broken. Alberto asked me how I had spent the summer and whether I had hidden in the coal cellar, and with that we both laughed. He remembered everything, without exception, that I had ever told him about myself. Then I asked him about his holiday. He immediately put on a weary and faraway expression and said that he had done nothing but look at the lake. He liked lakes, he said, because their water does not have the same violent colours and glaring light as that of the sea.

After we had sat for a short time in the café everything was just the way it had been before, and we laughed together at the stories I told him. He seemed very, very happy to be with me and I was happy too. I forgot how long a time I had waited for him in vain and told myself that if he had not been so busy he would surely have come to see me. I talked to him about my mother and father and the tax collector and the new arrivals at the boardinghouse. He made a sketch of me in his notebook while I was talking, then tore it up and made another. After that he sketched the lake where he had been staying, with himself rowing a boat and old ladies standing on the shore with little wiry-haired dogs holding their tails straight up in the air while they urinated against a tree.

We started to see each other once again almost every afternoon or evening. When I went upstairs to my room I asked myself if we were in love, without finding any answer. He never spoke of love and neither did I. I spoke only of my school and the boardinghouse and the books I had been reading. I thought of Alberto's slender hands sketching in his notebook, the curly black hair around his thin face, and his slight body in a light raincoat going about the city. I thought about them all day long, to the exclusion of everything else: first the hands, then the notebook, then the raincoat, and then again the notebook and the curly hair showing below his hat and the thin face and the hands. I read Xenophon to eighteen girls in a classroom newly repainted in green and decorated with a map of Asia and a portrait of the Pope; ate my meals in the boardinghouse dining room while the landlady paced up and down among the tables; took the bus to Maona every Saturday and felt more and more like an idiot because I had no interest in anyone or anything. I was no longer so sure that he loved me, although he went on bringing me books and chocolates and seemed to enjoy my company. But he said nothing about himself, and while I read Xenophon to my class or put the girls' marks down in my records, I could imagine only his slight figure going about its mysterious activities, wrapped in a flapping raincoat, following impulses and desires of which I was entirely ignorant. Then something like a fever would come over me. Once I had been a fairly good teacher and taken considerable interest in my pupils and their work. But now I felt not the least bit of affection for the eighteen girls in front of me; in fact, they bored me to the point of nausea and I could not even bear to look at them.

Francesca had come back from Rome in a very bad humour. I went to her house for dinner one night, meaning to leave early because Alberto might come to the boardinghouse to see me. It was an endless meal, with my aunt and uncle having a quarrel and Francesca sitting stubbornly silent in a stunning knitted black dress which made her look older than usual and very pale. After dinner my aunt took me up to her room and asked me what was the matter with Francesca. I told her that I didn't know, and all the time I was impatient to go away, but she clutched my hand and cried. She said that she couldn't understand Francesca at all, especially since Francesca had begun to wear nothing but black, with black hats that made her look so much older. She couldn't make out what Francesca had been up to at the school of dramatics or what she intended to do with herself next. Francesca had got herself engaged during the summer to a promising young man of good family, but then she had thrown him over. I felt the minutes passing by and feared that Alberto might be at the boardinghouse already, and here my aunt clutched my hand in hers and sniffled into her handkerchief.

It was late when I finally escaped. When I arrived at the boardinghouse they were locking the doors and the maid told me that the usual gentleman had come to see me, waited for a while in the drawing room, and then gone away. I went up to my room, got into bed, and cried. It was the first time in my life that I had cried over a man, and it seemed to me this must be a sign that I loved him. I thought how, if he asked me to marry him, I would say yes, and then we would always be together and even when he was out I would know where he was. But when I imagined our making love together I felt something like disgust and said to myself that I couldn't be in love with him after all. It was all very confusing.

But he never asked me to marry him, and we went on talking together like two good friends. He refused to speak of himself and always wanted me to do the talking. On days when I was in low spirits he seemed to be bored and I was afraid that he would never come to see me again. I forced myself to be gay and told him stories about the people at the boardinghouse and the landlady's screeching daughter, which we laughed at together. But when he went away I felt tired. I stretched out on my bed and thought back to all the things I used to imagine. Now I had become too idiotic to have any imagination. I absorbed his every word and tried to see if there was any love in it. I took his words and turned them over and over again in my mind. They seemed to have first one meaning and then another, until finally I let the whole thing go and dozed off.

Once Alberto told me that he had never done anything in earnest. He knew how to draw, but he was not a painter; he played the piano without playing it well; he was a lawyer but he did not have to work for a living and it didn't make much difference whether he turned up at his office or not. For this reason he stayed in bed all morning, reading. But often he had a feeling half of shame and half of satiety and thought he was going to stifle in his soft warm bed, with its yellow silk comforter. He said that he was like a cork bobbing on the surface of the sea, pleasantly cradled by the waves but unable to know what there was at the bottom. This was all he ever said about himself, except for the fact that he liked the country around the lakes. I absorbed these words and turned them over and over in my mind, but they amounted to very little beside the great stretches of mystery in his life, where only an old lady intent on her Sanskrit and a yellow silk comforter bobbed vaguely on the waves of my imagination.

While I was sitting there in the park it began to rain. I got up, went back to the café, and sat down at a small table near a window. Peering through the glass, I suddenly began to wonder whether anyone had heard my revolver shot. Our house is at the end of a quiet street, surrounded by a garden with trees. Quite possibly no one had heard it at all. This is the house of the old lady who studied Sanskrit; the bookcases are still full of Sanskrit tomes and the old lady's odour lingers on. I never saw the old lady for myself because she died before we were married, but I saw her ivory cigarette holder lying in a box, her bedroom slippers, her crocheted wool shawl, and her powder box, empty except for a wad of cotton. And everywhere there was her odour.

When Alberto's mother died he was a wreck. He found her one morning dead in her bed. That afternoon he was to take me to an art exhibition. Finally, when he didn't turn up, I phoned him and he told me that his mother was dead. I couldn't find much to say over the telephone, so I sat down and wrote him a letter. Sometimes I can manage such things fairly well, and this one came to me easily. I didn't go to the funeral because the old lady had left the express wish that no one should be invited, at least so Dr. Gaudenzi told me when I phoned him up to inquire.

A few days later I got a note from Alberto saying that he didn't feel like going out and would I come to his house to see him. My heart beat fast at the prospect. I found Alberto unshaven and with rumpled hair, wearing a pyjama jacket over his trousers. He tried to light the stove but only managed to stuff it with newspapers without getting it to burn. I succeeded in lighting it, and we sat down close by. He showed me a picture of his mother when she was young, a large, haughty woman with a big Spanish comb stuck in her hair. He spoke of her at great length, and I could not reconcile his description of her as a kindly and sensitive soul with either the young woman in the picture or the cantankerous old lady in bedroom slippers whom I had always imagined. I looked at the stove and the room and the garden outside with its high trees and the grapevine growing on the wall. Sitting with him there in his house, I felt quieter and more peaceful than I had felt for a long time, as if the feverishness and tension of the past few months had subsided.

I was so happy when I went away that I couldn't bear to stay alone in the boardinghouse and I went to see Francesca. But Francesca was in an abominable humour. She no sooner saw me than she complained of a headache and said she had no desire to listen to anyone's confidences. She lay there on her bed with a hot-water bottle and asked me to mend the lining of her coat because she had to go out. I mended it and went away.

Alberto didn't ask me to come to his house again. We went back to walking along the river and sitting for hours in cafés. Of his mother he spoke no more. He wore a black band on his coat sleeve, but he was making sketches in his notebook, including one of the two of us lighting the stove. When he went away I was left with a feeling of emptiness and stupor. For the life of me I couldn't make him out. I couldn't understand why he chose to spend so many hours with me, asking questions about the people in the boardinghouse and making sketches. Not a single word of love had ever passed between us. We went for long walks along the river or in the outskirts of the city, where lovers go, and yet we exchanged none of the words or gestures of love.

So it was that I finally spoke up and said that I loved him. I was weary of the burden of my secret; often in my boardinghouse room I could feel it growing within me until I thought I should burst, and all the time I was becoming more and more of an idiot, unable to take an interest in anyone or anything else. I had to find out whether he loved me, too, and whether one day we should be married. Knowing this was a necessity like eating and drinking, and all of a sudden it came to me that telling the truth was a necessity, too, no matter how difficult it seemed. And so I said that I loved him.

We were leaning up against the wall of a bridge. It was dark and wagons were passing slowly along the street with paper lanterns swinging under the horses' bellies, while birds whirred out of the tall rough grass beside the river. We had stood there silently for some minutes, watching darkness fall and the lights come on in the last scattered houses of the city. Alberto was telling me how as a little boy he had loved those paper lanterns and waited every year for the holiday when they were strung up on every balcony, only to be torn down, in melancholy fashion, the morning after. Then it was that I came out with the whole thing. I told him how I tormented myself waiting for him at the boardinghouse, how I couldn't concentrate on correcting my school papers, how I was gradually turning into a complete idiot, all because I loved him. I turned to look at him after I had spoken, and on his face there was a sad and frightened expression, which I knew meant he didn't love me at all. I began to cry and he pulled out a handkerchief to dry my tears. He was pale and frightened and said that he had never dreamed such a thing could happen. He enjoyed my company and considered me a good friend, but he simply didn't care for me that way. He said there was a woman he had been in love with for years. He couldn't marry her because she was already married, but he didn't think he could ever live with anyone else. He had made a great mistake to hurt me, but quite unintentionally, without ever dreaming that it could be so serious.

We went back to the city without speaking. When we said good night at the boardinghouse door he asked if he could come back the next day and I said I preferred never to see him again. "All right," he said as he started to go. I watched him walk away looking somehow humiliated, with the bent shoulders and slow, tired steps of a boy who has taken a beating.

I went up to bed without any dinner, leaving word with the maid to call Francesca and ask her if she could come over. Francesca had freshly plucked eyebrows and looked very handsome in her black knitted dress and a turban with a silk pendant. She sat on the edge of my bed, lit a cigarette, and said:

"Out with it!" But I could not speak through my tears, so she smoked and waited for me to pull myself together. "Still the same old guy?" she asked.

"Yes," I answered. She grimaced and blew out a mouthful of smoke.

"I simply can't see him," she said.

Little by little I told her the whole story. She stayed until midnight and we had to call the maid to open the front door and let her out. Francesca left me some sleeping pills, but I couldn't close my eyes all night long. Every now and then, as I began to doze off, Alberto's sad and frightened face surged up before me. I asked myself what I was going to do with my life and felt ashamed of the way I had spoken. Every word either one of us had said there on the bridge came back to haunt me.

Francesca returned the next morning and brought me some oranges. She sent the maid to the school to say that I had bronchitis and wrote a letter to my mother telling her that I wouldn't be home for the weekend because I was under the weather. She peeled an orange for me, but I couldn't eat it, so she ate it herself and told me to spend the day in bed. The only thing to do, she said, was to go and stay for two months with her at San Remo. I said I couldn't move on account of the school, and besides I hadn't the money. "Who gives a rap for that filthy school?" she said, and added that she had plenty of money for both of us and that we were leaving the very next day. When we got to San Remo she would lend me her low-necked pink tulle dress with the two blue roses on one shoulder. She pulled my suitcase out of the cupboard, wiped it off with a newspaper, and began to pack my clothes, then she went home to have lunch and do her own packing.

I stayed in bed for a while, thinking about the woman Alberto loved. I could see her standing motionless in front of me, staring at me out of cruel, stupid eyes that were set in a wide, heavily powdered face. She had a soft and abundantly curving figure and slender hands loaded with rings. Then this image faded away and I saw her as a weary hag with an outmoded wide-brimmed hat and a lean and hungry look about her. The weary hag was sorry for me, but I couldn't bear her presence in the room, and her compassionate expression froze me with horror. I asked myself what I was going to do with my life, and all the words exchanged between Alberto and myself flowed to and fro somewhere inside of me. My mouth was bitter and dry and my head throbbed.

The maid came up to tell me that the usual gentleman was downstairs in the drawing room. I got up, dressed, and went down. Alberto was sitting there with his briefcase on his knees and the shivery, cowed appearance of a little boy who had just had a caning. He said he hadn't been able to sleep, and I said

I hadn't either. We went out to a café together and sat at the far end of a dark, deserted room decorated with mirrors that had *Cinzano Vermouth* painted in red letters across them. They were playing billiards next door, and we could hear the knocking of balls and the hum of voices. Alberto said he couldn't get along without seeing me and that he had spent a very bad night thinking about how much he had hurt me. Since his mother had died the house was very lonely and the days when he didn't see me were empty and cold. I reminded him of the other woman. But he said she was often unkind to him and his life was entirely without joy. He felt stupid and useless, like a cork bobbing on the water.

I didn't go to San Remo. When Francesca came back I told her I didn't want to go. She lost her temper, threw the oranges on the floor, and kicked my suitcase over. The colonel's widow began to knock on the wall with her hairbrush. I told Francesca that San Remo was the last place in the world I wanted to go to, that I hated the violent colours and glaring light of the sea. I said I'd rather give up the ghost in my own room in the boardinghouse than board a train and go away. If you're in trouble, I told her, it's better to stew in your own juice in familiar surroundings. A change of air is positively fatal.

"Look out for yourself, then," she said. "And next time you're on your deathbed don't call me. I've better things to do." She jammed her turban on her head and looked at herself in the mirror while she buttoned up her coat and smoothed it over her hips.

When Alberto asked me to marry him I said yes. I asked him how he expected to live with me if he was in love with somebody else, and he said that if I loved him very much and was very brave we might make out very well together. Plenty of marriages are like that, he said, because it's very unusual for both partners to love each other the same way. I wanted to know a lot more about his feelings for me, but I couldn't talk to him for long about anything important because it bored him to try to get to the bottom of things and turn them over and over the way I did. When I began to speak of the woman he loved and to ask if he still went to see her, his eyes dimmed and his voice became tired and faraway and he said that she was a bad woman, that she had caused him a great deal of pain and he didn't want to be reminded of her.

So he said that we'd get married and we went on seeing each other. Now he held my hands and kissed me when we were alone in a café or beside the river, but he never set any definite month or day for our wedding. Finally I told him that we must go together to Maona and he must speak to my father about it. He didn't seem very enthusiastic, but he came. I wrote to my mother to take the garbage pail out of the kitchen and cook a good dinner for Saturday night because I was bringing someone with me.

We took the usual bus and Alberto made sketches of all the people on it. When we got to Maona my mother and father were somewhat taken aback, but Alberto reassured them by asking to speak to my father alone. They went into the smaller parlour together and my mother took in a brazier of coals to warm it up. Afterward my father came out looking very happy and we all drank marsala together. But my mother took me aside and half cried. Alberto seemed so old, she said, and then he only came up to my shoulder, whereas in her opinion a man ought to be taller than his wife. She asked me if I was sure I loved him, and when I said yes she took me up to her room to show me the bed and table linen she had set aside for the day of my marriage. Alberto spent the whole day chatting in the kitchen. My mother had taken the garbage pail away and bought two salt cellars so that the salt should not come to the table in a saucer. The vet and the tax collector dropped in after supper, and Father introduced Alberto as my fiancé. Alberto played a game of chess with the tax collector and then we drank some more marsala. Alberto became great friends with the tax collector, and before going back to the city that evening he promised to send him some Danish stamps for his collection.

Later that night, in my own room, when I was getting undressed and going to bed in the bed I had slept in ever since I was a child, a wave of terror and disgust came over me at the thought that soon Alberto and I would be married and make love together. I reassured myself with the idea that this was only because I had never made love before, but I remembered the slight disgust I felt every time he kissed me and wondered whether or not I really loved him. It's very difficult, I thought to myself, to know what we're really like inside. When it had seemed as if he were going out of my life I had felt so sad that I didn't want to go on living, and yet when he entered my life as he did just now when he talked to my father and mother I was filled with terror and disgust. But I came to the conclusion that I only needed to be a little braver because all girls must feel somewhat the same way. It's probably a mistake to follow every meandering of our feelings and waste time listening to every echo from within. That, in fact, is no way to live.

I stayed at Maona all day Sunday while my father went to the city to see Dr. Gaudenzi and find out something more about Alberto. He seemed quite pleased when he came back in the evening and said that he was glad I had found the proper sort of man and one of good social standing. My mother cried and said that marriage was a lottery, but he told her that she was being very silly and that women always have some excuse for shedding a few tears.

Before we were married, when we went for a walk or sat in a café, Alberto enjoyed my company even if he wasn't in love with me. He went out of his way to call on me; yes, even if it was raining he never failed to come. He sketched my face in his notebook and listened to what I had to say.

But after we were married he didn't sketch my face any more. He drew animals and trains, and when I asked him whether trains meant that he wanted to go away he only laughed and said no. He did go away, though, after we had been married just a month, and didn't turn up for ten days. One morning I found him packing his bag and he said he was going to the country with Augusto to revisit some of the scenes of their youth. He didn't ask me if I wanted to go; in fact, such a thought had apparently not even occurred to him. But this didn't particularly surprise me. Augusto and he had been boys together, and their friendship was so close that they had a way of talking to each other in something like a code which no outsider could decipher. And then he had said once that Augusto didn't like me. I wasn't too badly hurt, but I decided it was up to me to make myself agreeable to Augusto so that the next time they went anywhere together they'd ask me to come along. I, too, liked to wander about the countryside, but perhaps he didn't know it.

We had a sixteen-year-old girl called Gemma for a maid, the daughter of the shoemaker at Maona. She was very silly and had an unpleasant way of laughing through her nose. She had a notion that there were mice in the house, although I never saw any myself, and she used to sleep with her head under the covers for fear the mice would jump on her bed and eat her up. Finally she came back from Maona one day with a cat and talked to him while she did the cleaning. The cat used to run into the room where the old lady had died, and Gemma was afraid to go after him because she had a peasant belief that the old lady would pop out of a closet and strike her blind. The cat would sit purring on an armchair and Gemma would stand in the doorway trying to lure him out with scraps of cheese. I used to go into this room frequently myself, because I liked to picture the old lady in my imagination and catch the odour of her that lingered in the empty powder box and the tasselled curtains. Her armchair and footstool still stood beside the window, and her black dress and crocheted shawl were hanging in the closet.

Alberto's study was locked. Every time he went out of the house he locked the door and put the key in his pocket. When I asked him why, he said because there was a loaded revolver in the drawer of the desk. There was no lock on the drawer, so he locked the door of the room instead. With that he laughed and said he didn't want to put ideas in my head. For years and years he'd kept that revolver loaded in case he ever wanted to kill somebody, or perhaps commit suicide. Keeping it that way was such a habit that he was almost superstitious about it. He said Augusto kept a loaded revolver in the drawer of his desk too.

While Alberto was away I often stopped in front of that door. It wasn't on account of the revolver, I told myself, that he kept it locked. Perhaps there were letters and pictures in his desk. I was sorry that I hadn't anything to hide from him, that he knew everything there was to know about me. Before I met him my life had been colourless and dull. And after our marriage I had let everything go. I had stopped teaching and saw Francesca very infrequently. Ever since she had offered to take me to San Remo and I had let her down she had shown little desire to see me. I felt that she was making an effort not to say anything disagreeable and looked back sentimentally to the time when she used to bully and scold me instead of being distant and polite. The Gaudenzis used to ask Alberto and me to their house in the evening. They were always very nice and said they felt they had a share in our happiness because it was through them that we had met. But Alberto said they were stupid and uninteresting and he was always finding excuses to stay away. What he did like, however, was to have Augusto drop in. They would sit and talk in the study and I went to bed, because Alberto said that it embarrassed Augusto to see me.

A few days after Alberto had gone I met Augusto in the street. He was walking along with his overcoat collar turned up and his hands in his pockets, and he looked at me hard out of his strong stony face. I began to shake so that I couldn't say a word, and he nodded to me and walked hurriedly on. So now I knew that Alberto had lied when he told me he was going away with Augusto. I went back to the house and sat down by the stove and the cat crept up into my lap. Then it was that I thought for the first time that our marriage was a big mistake. I sat there stroking the cat and staring through the window at the leaves on the trees, which had turned pink in the glow of the sunset. All of a sudden I realized that I felt like a guest in this house. I never thought of it as mine, or the garden either, and I felt guilty whenever Gemma broke a plate, even if Alberto didn't say anything. Sometimes I half imagined that the old lady actually would pop out of a closet and chase Gemma and the cat and myself away. But where, then, could I feel at home? In my room at Maona my mother had begun to store potatoes and jars of tomato preserve. For a moment I wished I were back in the boardinghouse, with the landlady's hysterical daughter and the flowered hangings, boiling an egg over an alcohol flame.

Finally I had supper and went to bed. But it was cold and I lay there with my teeth chattering instead of going to sleep. Here in this bed we had made love for the first time when we came back from our fortnight's honeymoon on the lakes. I was disgusted and ashamed every time Alberto made love to me, but I imagined that all women must feel the same way at the start. I liked best to lie quietly and feel him sleeping beside me. I told him the way I felt about making love and asked him if other women felt the same way. He answered that he didn't know how the devil it was with women. The main thing for a woman was to have a baby, and for a man too. And I ought to cure myself of the habit of thinking about things so hard.

It had never occurred to me that he could lie. I had helped him pack his bag and made him take a blanket with him because I thought he might be cold in the inns and farmhouses where he said he would stay. He didn't want to take it, but I insisted. Then he left the house in a great hurry, saying that Augusto was waiting for him at the station.

I thought of our lovemaking and the tender, feverish words he whispered in my ear. Then he would fall asleep and I could hear his steady breathing beside me. I would lie awake in the darkness and try to remember every word he had said. I didn't care much for the lovemaking, but I enjoyed lying awake in the darkness and saying his words over and over to myself.

He hadn't gone away with Augusto, then. He had gone with that woman. Doubtless this wasn't the first time he had lied to me; doubtless they had gone on meeting even after he had decided to marry. When he said he was going to the office, perhaps he was going to see her instead. They were making love together and he said the same feverish words to her as he said to me. Then he probably lay quietly at her side and they sighed over the fact that they must live apart. I could see the woman standing motionless in the darkness before me, wearing a shiny silk dress and quantities of jewels. She yawned and pulled down her stockings with an indolent gesture. Then she disappeared, only to turn up again in a tall and masculine guise, striding along with a Pekinese dog in her arms.

Alberto stayed away ten days. The evening he came back he seemed tired and in a bad humour and he asked for a cup of very hot coffee. Gemma had already gone to bed, so I made the coffee and took it to him in our room. He drank it very slowly, staring at me all the while but making no motion to kiss me.

"You weren't with Augusto," I said. "Who were you with?"

He put the cup on the table, got up, and scratched his head. Then he took off his jacket and tie and threw them on the chair.

"I'm sleepy and tired," he said. "I don't feel like talking."

"Augusto was here all the time," I said. "I saw him on the street. Who were you with?"

"Alone," he answered. "I was alone." We got into bed and I put out the light. Suddenly Alberto's voice rose up out of the darkness.

"It was anything but a pleasant trip," he said. "I'd have done better to stay at home." He edged up to me and held me tight. "Don't ask any questions," he added. "I feel worn out and terribly sad. Just be silent and very, very still."

"Is she as bad as all that?" I asked.

"She's unfortunate," he said, running his hands over my body. "She can't help being unkind."

Hot, silent tears streamed down my cheeks. He touched my face with his hands and held me tighter.

"A perfectly hellish trip," he said, and I heard him laughing under his breath. "Don't ask any questions. Don't ever ask any questions. You're all I've got. Just remember that."

His hand lay on my shoulder, and I put out my hand to touch his thin, hot face. For the first time I wasn't disgusted when we made love.

A few months later Alberto went away again. I didn't ask him any questions. He was packing his bag in the study and I saw him put in a volume of Rilke. He used to read Rilke's poems out loud to me, too, in the evening. When he went out the door he said:

"I'll be back in a fortnight."

Then he turned the key in the lock, something he never forgot to do. I smiled at him as he left. The smile was still on my lips when I went back up the stairs and into my room, and I tried to keep it there as long as I could. I sat down in front of the mirror and brushed my hair, still with that silly smile on my face. I was pregnant and my face was pale and heavy. The letters I wrote to my mother had in them the same cowardly and idiotic smile. I hadn't gone to Maona for some time because I was afraid of the questions my mother might ask me.

"You're all I've got. Just remember that." Yes, I had remembered; indeed these words had helped me to go on living from day to day. But little by little they had lost their sweetness, like a prune stone that has been sucked too long. I didn't ask Alberto anything. When he came back to the house late at night I never asked him what he had been doing. But I had waited for him so long that a burden of silence had accumulated inside me. I looked in vain for something amusing to say to him so that he wouldn't be too bored with me. I sat knitting under the lamp while he read the paper, cleaning his teeth with a toothpick and scratching his head. Sometimes he sketched in his notebook, but he no longer drew my face. He drew trains and little horses galloping away with their tails streaming in the wind. And now that we had a cat he did cats and mice too. Once I told him that he should put my face on a mouse and his on a cat. He laughed and asked me why. So I asked him if he didn't think we two fitted into these roles. He laughed again and said there was nothing mouselike about me. Still he did draw a mouse with my face and a cat with his. The mouse was knitting, with a frightened and ashamed expression on its face, and the cat was angrily making a sketch in a notebook.

The evening after he had gone away for the second time Augusto came to see me and stayed quite late. He said that Alberto had asked him to keep me company sometimes in the evening while he was gone. I was taken aback and couldn't find anything to say. He sat there with his pipe between his teeth and an ugly grey wool scarf thrown around his neck, staring at me silently out of his square stony face with the black moustache. Finally I asked him if it was true that he didn't like me. He turned brick-red up to the eyebrows and then we had a good laugh together. That's how we started being friends. Sometimes when two people don't know what to say to each other some such trivial remark will turn the trick. Augusto told me that on general principles he didn't like anybody, that the only person he'd ever really liked was himself. Whenever he was in a bad humour, he said, he looked at himself in the mirror and began to smile and then he felt positively cheerful. I told him that I had tried smiling at myself in the mirror, too, but it didn't do any good. He asked me if I was in a bad humour very often and I said yes, I was. He stood in front of me with his pipe in his hand, blowing smoke out between his closed lips.

"That woman, Augusto…" I said. "What's she like?"

"What woman?" he asked.

"The woman who goes on trips with Alberto."

"Look here," he said. "It's no use talking about her. Besides, it doesn't seem right."

"I don't know anything about her," I said, "not even her name. And I torment myself trying to imagine her face."

"Her name is Giovanna," he said. "And her face—well, her face isn't anything special."

"Isn't she very beautiful?" I asked.

"How should I know?" he said. "I'm not an expert on beauty. Yes, she's beautiful, I suppose, when you come down to it. Or at least she was when she was young."

"Is she no longer young, then?"

"Not so very," he said. "But what's the point of discussing her?"

"Please," I said. "I'd like to be able to talk to you about her once in a while. It gets on my nerves to mope all by myself. I don't know a thing, you see. I didn't even know her name. I feel as if I were in the dark, as if I were blind and groping my way around, touching the walls and the objects in the room." My ball of yarn fell to the floor and Augusto bent over to pick it up.

"Why the devil did you two marry?" he asked.

"Yes," I said. "I made a mistake. He wasn't very keen on it, but he didn't stop to think. He doesn't like to think about important things. In fact, he hates people who are always searching inside themselves and trying to find some meaning to life. When he sees me sitting still and thinking he lights a cigarette and goes away. I married him because I wanted to know all the time where he was. But the way it turned out, he knows where I am—I'm just sitting here, waiting for him to come home—and I don't know where he is any more than I did before. He isn't really my husband. A husband is a man that—well, that you always know where he is. And if someone asks you: "Where's your husband?" then you ought to be able to answer without hesitation. Whereas I don't go out of the house for fear of meeting people I know and hearing them ask: "Where is he?" Because I shouldn't know what to answer. You may think I'm very silly, but I don't go out of the house."

"Why did you marry?" he repeated. "What got into you?" I began to cry. "It was a hell of an idea," he said, blowing the smoke out of his mouth and then staring at me in silence. He had a stubborn and gloomy expression on his face, as if he refused to be sorry for me.

"But where's Alberto?" I asked him. "Do you know where he is now?"

"No, I don't," Augusto answered. "I've got to go. Good night." He scraped the ashes out of his pipe with a matchstick and took his coat off the chair. Now his tall and solitary figure was standing in the doorway. "There isn't anything I can do about it," he said. "Good night."

I couldn't close an eye all night long. I imagined that Augusto had fallen in love with me and I was his mistress. Every day I would go to meet him at a hotel. I would come home very late and Alberto would search my face agonizingly to see where I had been. But when Augusto came to see me again a few evenings later I was ashamed of all the things I had imagined. He picked up my ball of wool when it fell to the floor, filled his pipe, lit it, scraped the ashes out of it with a matchstick, and paced up and down the room, while all the time I imagined how we would make love in a hotel room and blushed with shame at my own imaginings. I didn't speak again of Alberto and myself and neither did he. We didn't know what to talk about, and I had an idea he was as bored as I was. Only I was glad we had become friends, and I told Alberto as much when he came back. He didn't say anything, but he didn't look very pleased. He shouted and made a great fuss in the bathroom because the water was too hot and he couldn't find his shaving brush and the other things he was looking for. He came out of the bathroom freshly shaved, with a lighted cigarette in his mouth, and I asked him if this trip had been any more of a success than the one before. He said that it was a trip like any other and not worth talking about, that he had gone on business to Rome. I said I wished he wouldn't go away again before the baby was born because I was afraid of what might happen if I had pains during the night when I was all alone. He said I wasn't the first woman in the world to have a baby and if I was so nervous it was just too bad. We didn't say anything more, but I cried over my knitting, and then he went out, slamming the door behind him.

Augusto came to the house that evening and I kept him in the drawing room, where Alberto told him that he'd been on a business trip to Rome and thanked him for keeping me company. A little later Gemma called me into the kitchen to look over the household accounts, and when I came back the two men had gone into the study. I wondered whether to join them there or to wait in the drawing room, and after considerable hesitation I decided that there was nothing so strange about my going to join them. I picked up my knitting and started to go into the study, but the door was locked and I could hear Alberto saying: "It's quite useless." What did he mean? I sat down in the drawing room and began to count stitches. I felt tired and heavy and the baby stirred inside of me. Then and there I wanted to die with my baby, to escape from this torment and not feel anything more. I went to bed and to sleep but woke up when Alberto came in.

"I'm not afraid any more; I only want to die," I said.

"Go to sleep and don't be silly," he answered. "I don't want you to die."

"What difference would it make to you?" I asked him. "You have Augusto and Giovanna. You don't need me. You don't need the baby either. What will you do with a baby anyhow? You've grown old without ever having a baby and you got along perfectly well without it."

"I'm not so old," he said with a laugh. "I'm only forty-four."

"You are old, though," I said. "You have a lot of grey hair. You got along without a baby for forty-four years. What will you do with one now? It's too late for you to get used to having a baby crying about the house."

"Please don't say such silly things," he said. "You know perfectly well I'm anxious to have this baby."

"Why didn't you ever have one with Giovanna?"

Out of the darkness he gave a deep sigh.

"I've asked you not to talk about that person."

I sat bolt upright in the bed.

"Don't say 'that person.' Say 'Giovanna.'"

"As you like."

"Say 'Giovanna.'"

"Giovanna, then."

"Why didn't you ever have a baby together?"

"I don't think she ever wanted to have a baby by me."

"No? Then she can't love you very much."

"I don't think she does love me very much."

"I don't love you either. No one can love you. Do you know why? Because you have no courage. You're a little man who hasn't enough courage to get to the bottom of anything. You're a cork bobbing on the surface, that's what you are. You don't love anybody and nobody loves you."

"You don't love me, then?" he asked.

"No."

"When did you stop loving me?"

"I don't know. Some time ago."

Once more he sighed.

"It's all too bad," he said.

"Alberto," I said, "tell me where you were these last few days."

"In Rome, on business."

"Alone or with Giovanna?"

"Alone."

"Do you swear it?"

"I don't want to swear," he said.

"Because it isn't true. That's why. You were with Giovanna. Where did you go? To the lakes? Did you go to the lakes?"

He put on the light, got up, and took a blanket out of the cupboard.

"I'm going to sleep in my study. Both of us will get more rest that way."

He stood there in the middle of the room with the blanket over his arm, a slight figure in rumpled blue pyjamas, with his hair in disorder and a look of weariness and distress in his eyes.

"No, Alberto, don't go away; I don't want you to go away." I was weeping and trembling and he came over and stroked my hair. I took his hand and kissed it. "It's not true that I don't love you," I said. "I love you more than you can possibly know.

I couldn't live with any other man. I couldn't make love with Augusto or with anybody else. I like making love with you. I'm your wife. I'm always thinking of you when you're away. I can't think of anything else, no matter how hard I try. It's idiotic of me, I know, but I can't help it. I think of every single thing that's happened to us since the day we first met. I'm glad I'm your wife."

"Then everything's all right," he said, picking up the blanket. He went to sleep in the study, and it was a long time before we slept together again.

It was dark when I left the café. The rain had stopped, but the pavement was still glistening. I realized that I was very tired and I had a burning feeling in my knees. I walked about the city for a while longer, then I took a tram and got off in front of Francesca's house. There were bright lights in the drawing room, and I could see a maid passing a tray. Then I remembered that it was Wednesday, and Wednesday was Francesca's day for receiving her friends at home, so I didn't go in. I went on walking. My feet were heavy and tired, and there was a hole in the heel of my left stocking, where my shoe rubbed against the bare skin and gave me pain. Sooner or later, I thought, I'd have to go home. I shivered and a wave of nausea came over me, so I went back to the park. I sat down on a bench and slipped off my shoe to look at the sore spot on the back of my heel. The heel was swollen and red; a blister had formed and broken and now it was bleeding. Couples were embracing each other on the park benches, and in the shadow of the trees an old man lay asleep under a dark green coat.

I shut my eyes and remembered certain afternoons when I used to take the baby out in the park. We used to walk very,

very slowly and I would give her warm milk out of a thermos bottle I carried in my bag. I had an enormous bag where I used to put all the baby's things: a rubber bib and one of towelling and some little raisin biscuits that she especially liked, sent by my mother from Maona. Those were long afternoons I used to spend in the park, turning around to watch the baby follow me in her velvet-edged hood, her little coat with the velvet buttons, and her white leggings. Francesca had given her a camel that swayed its head as it walked. It was a lovely camel with a gold-embroidered red cloth saddle, and it swayed its head in a very wise and appealing way. Every other minute the camel would get tangled up in its string and fall and we had to set it on its feet again. Then we walked slowly on among the trees in the warm, humid sunshine. The baby's mittens would come off and I would lean over to pull them on and blow her nose and then carry her when she was tired.

I would go home for the night, I thought, and to the police station in the morning. I didn't know where the police station was, so I'd have to look it up in the telephone book. I'd ask them to let me tell the whole story, from the very first day, including certain details which might seem trivial enough but had considerable importance. It was a long story, but they'd have to let me talk. I tried to imagine the face of the man who would listen to me, and I saw him, with a moustache and an olive complexion, sitting behind a desk. I shivered again and suddenly I wanted to phone Augusto and Francesca and ask them to go to the police station for me. Or else I might write a letter to the police and wait for them to come and pick me up at home. Of course they'd put me in jail, but I couldn't exactly imagine how that would be. All I could see was the police station and a man with a long, shiny, olive-skinned face behind a desk. When he laughed it made me shiver, and then everything was a blank, days and years tumbling out of my life that had no connection with the days and years that had been filled with the baby and Alberto and Augusto and Francesca and Gemma and the cat and my father and mother at Maona. It didn't matter at this point whether or not I went to jail. Everything that mattered had happened already, for everything that mattered was Alberto at the moment when I shot him and he fell heavily across the table and I closed my eyes and ran out of the room.

Our little girl was born three years ago on January eleventh at three o'clock in the afternoon. I trailed around the house in a wrapper, moaning with pain, for two whole days while Alberto followed me with a frightened look on his face. Dr. Gaudenzi came to take care of me, bringing a young and obnoxious nurse who called Alberto "Daddy." The nurse had a fight with Gemma in the kitchen because she said the kettles were dirty. They needed lots of hot water, and Gemma was terrified by my moans and groans, besides having a stye in her eye that made her particularly unintelligent. My father and mother came too. I wandered about the house making senseless remarks to the effect that they must hurry up and help me to get rid of that infernal baby. Then I was so dead tired I went to bed and fell asleep for a minute, only to wake up shrieking with pain until the nurse told me I'd get a goitre from straining my throat that way. I had forgotten the baby and Alberto, and all I wanted was to go to sleep and stop suffering. I no longer wanted to die; in fact, I was scared to pieces of dying and asked nothing more than to live. I begged everyone to tell me when the pain would be over, but it lasted a very long time, while the nurse went to and fro with kettles of water, my mother huddled in her black dress in a corner, and Alberto held my hand. But I didn't want his hand; I only bit the sheet and tried, regardless of the baby, to get rid of that terrible pain in my middle.

Then the baby was born and suddenly all my pain was gone. I raised my head to look at her as she lay there naked and red between my legs, and Alberto leaned over me with relief and joy on his face while I felt happier than I had ever felt in my life, with the pain gone from my body, leaving me with a sense of glory and peace.

My mother put the baby in bed beside me, wrapped in a white shawl with her two cold, red fists and her damp, bald little head sticking out. I saw Gemma's face leaning over with a glorious smile, and my mother's face had a glorious smile on it, too, while the baby's feeble whimpering in the shawl filled me with joy.

Everyone said I ought to sleep, but now I didn't want to. I talked incessantly and asked how the baby looked and what kind of a nose and mouth and forehead she had. They closed the shutters and took the baby away, leaving Alberto alone with me, and we laughed together over the stye in Gemma's eye and the nurse's way of calling him "Daddy." Alberto asked me if I still wanted to die, and I told him that was the last thing I wanted to do, but I did want a glass of orange juice because I was thirsty. He went to get the juice and brought it to me on a tray, holding up my head while I drank it and planting a gentle kiss on my hair.

The baby was very ugly at first, and Alberto called her the "little toad." Every time he came back from outside the first thing he asked was: "What's the little toad up to?" Then he stood with his hands in his pockets, looking down into her cradle. He even bought a camera to take pictures of her as soon as she was slightly better to look at.

My father and mother went away after a few days, and when my mother asked me at the last minute whether I was happy I told her I most certainly was. She sent me a big box of woollens for the baby and a pair of socks she had knitted for Alberto, while my father sent a case of wine. It made them happy to think that all was going well with me, and my mother wrote to me that because Alberto was thin and had no appetite I should see to it that he didn't overwork and that the baby didn't disturb his sleep.

Probably my mother thought that we would sleep together again now that the baby was born, but he went right on sleeping in the study, as he had ever since coming back from his last trip, and I kept the baby's crib near my bed. But I couldn't sleep very well because I got up frequently to see how the baby was sleeping and whether she was hot or cold and to listen to her regular breathing. After the first few months she became very bad and woke up crying all the time, until I picked her up and rocked her in my arms. I was afraid that Alberto would hear her, so I picked her up in a hurry and walked up and down the room, singing to her in a low voice. That way she got worse and worse. She liked to have me rock her and would apparently fall asleep in my arms with her eyes shut and her breathing even, but just as soon as I put her down in the crib she started crying again. As a result I was sleepy all day long.

I didn't have much milk to give her, so I stuffed myself with food until I was quite fat. But the baby stayed thin, and when I took her out in her carriage I used to look at the other babies and ask how old they were and how much they weighed and feel ashamed because mine wasn't as fat and strong as the rest. I hastened to weigh her immediately after every time I gave her the breast and every Saturday, without her clothes on, just before her bath. I kept a notebook, where I wrote down in red ink her weekly weight and in green her increase of weight after every feeding. Saturdays I got up with a pounding heart, hoping that she would be a little heavier than the week before, but often she wasn't and I was plunged into despair. Alberto got angry with me about this and said that he had been a thin baby himself. He teased me about the notebook and about the way my hands trembled when I was dressing or undressing the baby, the way I upset the talcum powder and rushed breathlessly around the howling baby. He made a sketch of me with my mouth full of safety pins and a breathless, frightened air about me, letting the belt of my open wrapper drag on the floor, and wearing my hair in a net because I didn't feel like combing it.

I didn't let Gemma touch the baby; in fact, I was distressed whenever she went over to whisper sweet nothings in her ear and to shake her rattle with damp, red hands. I didn't even like to see Augusto come into the room because I was afraid he might bring in some germs from outside. Augusto lived with a sister who had a small child, and I feared he might be the carrier of whooping cough or measles. Moreover, I was ashamed to have Augusto tell me that his sister's child was fat and strong.

When the baby was two or three months old Alberto began to take pictures of her: in her bath, on the table, bareheaded, and with her cap on. For a while this gave him great amusement and he bought a better camera and an album with a flowered cover where he pasted in the pictures with the dates when they were taken and a phrase of comment in red ink below.

But this amusement soon palled, because he was a man who tired quickly of everything. One day he said he was going to visit some friends who had a villa on one of the lakes, and I saw him pack the volume of Rilke in his bag. He locked the study door, as he never forgot to do, and after he had gone I looked at the photograph album on the drawing-room table, which had remained only half filled after he lost his interest in photography. It depressed me to see the empty black pages, with the last picture of the baby holding her rattle, and written in red ink underneath it: "We begin to play."

There was only one thing in life that Alberto didn't tire of, I reflected, and that was his passion for Giovanna. Because I was sure he had gone with her to the lake and they were sitting on a bench beside the water reading Rilke together. He had long ago given up reading Rilke with me in the evening and taken to reading a book or newspaper to himself, picking his teeth or scratching his head at intervals and never saying a word about what he was thinking. I wondered if this might be my fault, although I had always listened attentively and told him I liked Rilke's poems, even when they bored me. How had Giovanna managed to hold his interest for all these years? Perhaps she never showed that she loved him, but tormented and deceived him so that he had not a moment of peace and could not possibly forget her. I went over to the cradle and felt sorry for the baby because I was the only one who really loved her. I picked her up and unbuttoned my dress, and while I was nursing her I thought that when a woman has her baby in her arms nothing else should matter.

I began to wean the baby when she was six months old and tried to feed her a thin porridge to which she did not take at all. Dr. Gaudenzi was very kind about coming to see her, but occasionally he lost his patience and said that I took things too hard and couldn't seem to relax. There he was quite right. Every time the baby had a touch of fever I went into a panic and didn't know what I was doing. I took her temperature every five minutes, looked up in a book all the diseases that she could possibly have, stopped eating my meals and combing my hair and couldn't sleep at night. At times like these my temper was constantly on edge and I would shout at Gemma as if everything were her fault. Then, when the baby's fever went down, I returned to reason, felt sorry for the way I had treated her, and gave her a handsome present. For a while afterward I didn't particularly want to see the baby. I almost loathed everything connected with her: the rattle, the talcum powder, the diapers, and all the rest, and only wished I could read a novel or go to the theatre with friends. But I hadn't any friends, and when I opened a book it bored me and I went back to reading about infants' diseases and diet.

One evening while I was cooking the porridge Francesca turned up at the house. She was hatless and had no makeup on her face, while a lock of hair tumbling over her forehead and the raincoat thrown over her black dress gave her a gloomy and defiant air. She told me she had quarrelled with her mother and asked me if I could put her up for the night. I told Gemma to make up the couch in the drawing room. Francesca sat down, puffed at a cigarette, and watched me give the baby her porridge, which the baby spat out as soon as I got it in her mouth.

"I couldn't stand a baby," said Francesca. "If ever I had a baby I'd kill myself, for sure."

Alberto was in his study and I went to tell him that it was Francesca and that she had come to stay with us because there was something wrong at home.

"Good," he said. He was reading a German book on Charles V and writing notes in the margin.

I put the baby to bed. Francesca was stretched out on the drawing-room couch, smoking another cigarette and looking as if the place had always been hers. She had taken off her garters and hung them over the back of an armchair, and she flicked the ashes from her cigarette on to the rug.

"Did you know he was unfaithful to you?" she asked.

"Yes, I know that."

"Don't you care?"

"No."

"Why don't you leave him?" she asked. "Let's go for a trip somewhere. He's a little rat of a man. What good is he to you?"

"I love him," I said, "and then there's the baby."

"But he's deceiving you. He does it in the most blatant sort of way. I see them together sometimes. She has a behind like a cauliflower. Nothing much to look at."

"Her name is Giovanna," I said.

"Leave him, I say. What good is he to you?"

"So you've seen her, have you? What's she like?"

"Well … She doesn't know how to dress. They walk along very slowly. I see them all the time."

"Why did you say she has a behind like a cauliflower?"

"Because that's what it's like, that's all. It's round, I mean, and she shakes it when she walks. But what do you care?"

Francesca took all her clothes off and walked up and down the room. I locked the door.

"Are you afraid that rat will see me?" she said. "Lend me a nightgown, will you?" I brought her a nightgown and she put it on. "I rattle around in it," she said. "You've got fat."

"I'll lose weight now that the baby's weaned."

"I don't want any children," she said. "I don't want to get married. Do you know why I fell out with my mother? Because there was a man they wanted me to marry. He works for a shipping company. They've been trying for ages to marry me off. But I've had enough. I'm not going home. I'll take a room somewhere and look for a job. I've had enough of family. I don't want to be tied to a husband, either. Just to get myself let down the way you are? Not me! I like going to bed with a man. But I'm all for variety. A couple of times with one man is enough for me."

I listened to her with astonishment.

"You've had lovers, then?" I asked.

"Of course I have," she said, laughing. "Are you shocked?"

"No," I said, "but I don't understand how you can do it."

"Do what?"

"Change all the time."

"You don't understand?"

"No."

"Oh, I've had a lot of men," she said. "First, one in Rome, when I was trying to get on the stage. I broke that off when he asked me to marry him. I was tired of him, anyhow; quite ready to throw him out of the window. But I still took such things seriously. 'What kind of a girl am I?' I said to myself. 'I must be a bitch if I like to change so often.' Words have a way of scaring us when we're young. I still thought I ought to marry and be like everyone else. Then little by little I learned to make life less of a tragedy. We have to accept ourselves for what we are."

"And other people for what they are, too," I said. "That's why I have to put up with Alberto. And then I shouldn't like to change."

She burst out laughing and kissed me.

"Am I a bitch?" she asked.

"No, you're not a bitch," I said. "But you'll be alone in your old age."

"What the devil do I care about that? I'll kill myself when I'm forty. Or else you'll walk out on this little rat and we'll live together."

I kissed her and went into my room. My head was whirling with a medley of words: rat, cauliflower, bitch, accepting people for what they are, and killing oneself. I could see Alberto walking slowly along with Giovanna the way he used to walk with me before we were married. Now we never went for a walk together at all. Finally I went to bed. I had a strong urge to go into the study and stretch out beside him in his bed. I wanted to put my head on his shoulder and ask him why we never went for any more walks. I wanted to tell him that I could never change to another man. But I was afraid he might think I was there just in order to make love with him, so I stayed in my own bed, waiting for sleep to come.

Francesca stayed with us three weeks. I was very happy all this time, and it did me good to talk to her. I was no longer so nervous over the baby's diarrhoea, and when I did show some nervousness she teased me out of it. Sometimes she persuaded me to leave the baby with Gemma while we went to a moving picture together. It was fun to get up in the morning, find Francesca wandering about the house in a long white satin wrapper and cold cream on her face, and pass the time of day with her until it was time for lunch. It was, in fact, a relief to have her to talk to. I realized then how little Alberto and I had to say to each other any more and how I practically never felt that I could tell him what I was thinking. When he was at home he spent most of his time in the study, which was in a state of complete disorder because he wouldn't let anyone tidy it up.

Gemma made his bed and swept, under his strict supervision, but that was all she was allowed to do. He forbade her to touch either his desk or books, with the result that everything was covered with dust and the place gave out a bad smell.

On his desk Alberto kept a picture of his mother and a plaster bust of Napoleon that he had modelled himself when he was sixteen years old. It looked very little like Napoleon, but it was a good technical job. Then he had a fleet of miniature ships which he had built as a little boy, copies exact down to every last detail. Of these he was very proud, particularly of a tiny sailing boat with a pennant flying from the mast. He asked Francesca into his study to admire them and insisted that she examine the sailing boat carefully. Then he showed her his library and read some of Rilke's poems out loud. With Francesca he was very agreeable and in fact put himself out to please her as he always did when he came up against somebody new. And then I fancied that Francesca somewhat frightened him. It even occurred to me that Giovanna tyrannized him by fright too. I was the only person he wasn't afraid of, and perhaps that was the root of the whole trouble. No, he certainly wasn't afraid of me.

Francesca sent me to her house for some clothes. My aunt was there and burst into tears as soon as she saw me. She asked me any number of questions, which I didn't know how to answer. She couldn't understand why Francesca wouldn't consider the man from the shipping company, who was handsome and very much of a gentleman as well. She had never understood what Francesca wanted to do with her life, or anything else about her.

"It's this younger generation," she said, weeping and rubbing her face with her wet handkerchief. I tried to tell her that

Francesca was still young and had plenty of time ahead of her in which to find a man more to her liking. Then she told me that she didn't care for the way Francesca behaved with men, flirting with them and keeping three or four on her string at a time. I don't think for a moment that it ever remotely occurred to her that Francesca had any lovers. She did her best to understand, but the task was quite beyond her. I thought how all of us are always trying to imagine what someone else is doing, eating our hearts out trying to find the truth and moving about in our own private worlds like a blind man who gropes for the walls and the various objects in a room. Then I wrapped up Francesca's clothes and went away.

Francesca was plucking her eyebrows in the kitchen, looking into a mirror which she held in one hand. Gemma stood there gaping at her until Francesca grimaced and said:

"Run me a bath, will you, my girl?"

Gemma hurried away, laughing, and Francesca pulled her clothes out of the bundle and scrutinized them carefully, turning them over and over in her hands. I asked her whether she was ever going home.

"No," she said dryly. "Don't ask me again."

I was preparing to give the baby her first orange juice and feeling a little sentimental about it. I was glad that she was turning into a big girl and starting to eat grown-up food.

"What a lot of fuss," said Francesca as she saw me boiling a spoon. "And when she's older she'll just be a pain in the neck the way I am to my mother. Families are a stupid invention. No marriage for me, thank you!"

I was almost jealous of Francesca. Alberto was always making up to her and sketching her face. She treated him with scorn, but when he began to make sketches of her in his notebook she came down from her high horse. In the evening Alberto would call us into his study to hear Rilke's poems and Augusto would come to join us. I decided that they might make a good match, but when I said as much to Francesca she replied that Augusto looked like a justice of the peace with his heavy moustache and scarf and the shirt sleeves that stuck out below those of his jacket. Even the man from the shipping company was a cut above him. But every time Augusto came she powdered her nose and debated in front of the mirror as to whether she should wear her best necklace.

Finally Francesca sold some of her jewels and rented a one-room apartment. She said she was going to look for a job, but meanwhile she did nothing in particular except try her hand at painting, because she claimed to have lost interest in the stage. She painted strange pictures with great splotches of colour and everything in them but the kitchen stove: houses, skulls, knights in armour, and invariably the moon. She wore a long grey linen smock and painted all day long and said that she didn't have a lover.

I was still very busy with the baby. She was just starting to walk and I had to trail her all over the house to make sure she didn't fall. She cried every time I left her alone, and I had to take her with me, even into the bathroom. She was given to tantrums and never wanted to eat her meals. I had to play with her at mealtime and get the food down without her knowing it. She staggered around the room, from chair to chair, playing with the cat and my sewing basket, and I followed her with a bowl in my hand, waiting for the right moment to slip a spoon into her mouth.

Until she was a year old the baby had lead-grey eyes, but then I noticed flecks of brown coming into them. She had very fine blonde hair which I combed back and tied with a ribbon. She was still thin and pale and not what you could call beautiful; her eyes were dull and often had dark circles around them. Eating and sleeping simply did not interest her. She cried every evening before going to sleep, and I had to walk up and down the room singing lullabies. She always wanted to hear the same thing, a French song I had learned from my mother:

> Le bon roi Dagobert
> A mis sa culotte à l'envers!
> Le bon Saint Éloi
> Lui dit: O mon roi,
> Votre Majesté
> Est mal culotté.

I used to tie a red cloth around the lamp and sing as I paced up and down with the baby in my arms. When I left the room I felt exhausted, as if from a battle. Very often I had no sooner gone out than her feeble and plaintive cry followed me and I had to go back and start all over again. She couldn't stand Alberto and cried whenever he picked her up, and he in his turn said that I had spoiled her and made her into a perfect little pest. Alberto was seldom at home and went on a number of his usual trips. When he was at home he shut himself up in the study with Augusto. But at this point I didn't particularly care what they were talking about, whether it was Giovanna or something quite different. All that mattered to me was to see the baby eat her supper until the picture of a chick emerging from the egg at the bottom of her bowl was uncovered and the bowl was empty. I remembered Alberto's telling me that a baby was the main thing in a woman's life and in a man's too. This was all very true for a woman, I reflected, but not for a man. Alberto's habits had not changed an iota since our baby was born. He took the same trips, made the same sketches in his notebook, went on jotting down phrases on the margins of his books, and continued to walk down the street at the same brisk pace as before, with a cigarette stuck between his lips. He was never upset if the baby was pale or hadn't eaten her supper. He didn't really know what she was supposed to eat, and perhaps he had not even noticed that her eyes were changing colour.

I thought I was cured of my jealousy and that I didn't care to know whether he was seeing Giovanna or not. I had borne his child and that was enough. The days when I had waited for him in the boardinghouse and trembled at the mere thought of his coming now seemed so remote that I could hardly believe they belonged to the same existence. Occasionally he called me into the study to make love, but I was always on the alert for the baby's cry and didn't stop to wonder how much I enjoyed it. He didn't ask me, either, and I came to the conclusion that our marriage was no better and no worse than the run-of-the-mill variety.

One day I went for a walk with the baby. Francesca had given her the camel, and this was the first time we were taking it out. The camel was handsome and swayed its head in such a way that people stopped to look at it. We went slowly in the warm sunshine, and I was very cheerful because the baby had drunk her milk and eaten two ladyfingers. The camel kept falling down and I would stoop to pick it up and dust its red cloth saddle.

Then I saw Alberto crossing the street with a woman. All that I could see of her was that she was tall and wore a mouton fur piece. I picked the baby and the camel up in my arms and hurried back home. The baby struggled and cried because she wanted to walk, but I held her tight until I came to the door. Then I told Gemma to take off her coat and keep her in the kitchen while I wrote a letter. I shut the drawing-room door and sat down on the sofa. I had thought of Giovanna so often and pictured her as having a wide, immobile face that this image had lost all power to hurt me. Now I had to adjust myself to the sight of her as a tall woman with a mouton fur piece, and I clenched my teeth to put down the pain I felt inside. They had been walking very slowly, just as Francesca said. He had left the house at three o'clock that afternoon, saying that he had some long-neglected law cases to attend to at the office. And when I saw them it was half past four. Obviously he lied to me all the time without a qualm, without a single muscle of his face betraying him. He had taken his hat off the rack, slipped on his raincoat, and gone out at his usual brisk pace.

Darkness was coming on when he returned to the house. I was still lying on the sofa while the baby played with the cat and Gemma set the dining-room table. Alberto went into his study and called out to me to follow. When I looked at his face I knew that he had seen me too. He looked as if he had been through a wringer, and he had hardly any voice at all.

"We can't go on living together," he said.

"No," I replied.

"It's not your fault," he said. "You've done everything a woman could do. You've been a perfect dear and given me a great deal. But perhaps you were right to say that I was too old to get used to having a wife and child. I'm still tied to my past. And I can't go on." He looked at me and waited for me to speak. Then, when I said nothing, he continued: "It's not just what you think. I shan't go and live with anyone else. I need to be alone. That's the way I want to live from now on. I hate this perpetual lying to you. I have too much respect for you to tell you lies. It makes me feel oppressed and guilty. I want to be alone and at peace."

"You're not going to live with Giovanna?" I asked.

"No," he said, "I swear to that."

"Not that I care," I added. "What can it matter to me if we're not together? Why don't you want to live with her, though?"

"I don't, that's all. She has a husband and son. We met too late. That's the way it always happens. But I'm very much attached to her, and it disgusts me to live with another woman."

"It disgusts you?"

"Yes."

"It disgusts you to live with me? I disgust you?"

"No," he said. "That's not it. It disgusts me to tell so many lies."

"'It disgusts me to live with another woman,' that's what you said, isn't it?"

"Don't plague me. Don't plague me that way, I beg of you. I don't remember what I said. I only meant that I don't think it's fair for me to tie you down. You're still young and you might find happiness with another man."

"But there's the baby. You remember that, don't you?"

"I'll come to see you often. You must stay here and I'll take a room outside. I'll come, never fear. We'll always be friends."

"We shan't be friends at all. We never have been. You've never been even a friend to me or a husband either. But I shouldn't be happy with another man. If I were to make love with another man I'd always see your face. I shall never be able to get away from that. It's not so simple as you think."

"I never said it was simple. You'll have to be very brave. But you're honest and courageous, too. That's what attracted me to you. Because I'm neither one nor the other. Oh, I know myself very well."

"And Giovanna?" I asked. "What's she like?"

"Don't plague me," he said. "If you knew how difficult it is for me to speak of her to you. It's something that's been going on for years and years, and I don't really know what it's about. Eleven years it's lasted and we've become very close to one another. We've felt very unhappy and suffered together and made each other suffer. She's been unfaithful and lied to me, and we've said all sorts of cruel things to each other and given up the affair completely. Then we've come together again, and every time, even after so many years, it's like something brand new. She suffered a lot when I married you. I was glad to know that she was suffering on my account. God knows I'd suffered often enough on hers. I thought it would go smoothly and then I could forget her. But when we two started living together it was terribly painful for me to be with you instead of with her. I wanted to have a child with you just as she had one with another man. I wanted to talk about 'my child' when she talked about hers and to have a private life of my own which should be just as mysterious to her as hers was to me. We've said good-bye so many times, only to start all over again. Now I just can't live with you any longer. I'll take a room somewhere and live by myself. Then I'll come often to see the baby. Who knows, we may really be better friends than we are now. Perhaps it won't be so hard for me to talk with you about a lot of things."

"Very well," I said. "As you like."

"You're a fine girl," he murmured. He looked exhausted, and his voice was worn out from having talked for so long about himself. He didn't want any supper and neither did I, so we had a cup of tea in the study.

Then I had to put the baby to sleep by singing her the song of *Le bon roi Dagobert*. It took her a long time to fall off. Finally I laid her in her crib, covered her up, and stood there looking down at her for a while. Alberto came in to look at her, too, for a minute and then went away.

I got undressed and looked in the mirror at my naked body, which now belonged to no man. I was free to do what I wanted. I could go for a trip with Francesca and the baby, for instance. I could make love with any man who happened to catch my fancy. I could read books and see new places and discover how other people lived. In fact, I ought to do all of these things. I had made a mess of my life, but there was still time to set it straight. If I made enough of an effort I could turn into quite a different woman. After I had gone to bed I lay for a long time staring into the darkness, and I felt the growth of a new cold-blooded resolution inside me.

The next day I wrote to ask my mother if she would keep the baby at Maona for a while, as she had said for some time that she wanted to do. My father came to the city and took Gemma and the baby away with him. The baby struggled in Gemma's arms and called for me. I went away from the window and stuck my fingers in my ears in order not to hear her cries. I had to have a rest and to get away from *Le bon roi Dagobert*. I went to see Francesca and found Augusto there. This wasn't the first time I had come upon them together and I began to think they might be lovers. Francesca was painting with an expression of concentration on her face while Augusto sat reading and smoking his pipe at the table.

"I've seen the cauliflower, do you know?" I announced.

Francesca looked at me in a puzzled way; then she caught on and burst out laughing.

"She doesn't dress well, does she?" she said.

"I don't know," I said. "She had on a mouton fur piece."

Augusto knit his brows because he didn't understand.

"Alberto and I are breaking up," I added.

"At last!" Francesca exclaimed. She took me into the bathroom and laid her hands on my shoulders. "See that you're smart now and get every penny out of him you can," she said. "Always be smart, remember. That ratty little man."

Augusto went out with me when I left. It was a clear, windy afternoon and heavy, white cloud scudded across the sky. He asked me if I felt like walking and I said I did. We walked haphazardly along the river and then up a weedy alley to a large square overlooking the city. We could hear distant train and factory whistles, and trams went by below us, ringing their bells and raising sparks on the overhead wire among the leaves of the trees. The wind ruffled my hair and whipped up Augusto's scarf across his distracted and indifferent face. In the middle of the square there was a bronze statue of a woman holding a sheaf of wheat, and we sat down on the stone pedestal. I asked Augusto if he was in love with Francesca and he said no, but I didn't believe it. It floated into my mind that when it was all over between them I might make love with Augusto, and for some reason this prospect left me very calm. Looking at his black moustache, his nose reddened from the cold, and his hard, lonely face, I hadn't the slightest desire to make love with him. But there was plenty of time ahead and I might change my mind.

"So you and Alberto have decided to part company," he said.

"No," I said. "It's his idea, really. Perhaps it's all for the best."

He filled his pipe with tobacco from his pouch, which he was holding between his knees, and looked down at the ground, shaking his head.

"There's just one thing I'd like to ask you," I said. "Do you ever see Giovanna?"

"Every now and then," he said. "Why?"

"I wish you'd tell her to come and see me some day. Not for the reason you may think. I don't want to make a scene or arouse her pity. I just want to speak to her, that's all. After that I think my mind would be at rest. I've thought about her so often and tried to imagine what we'd say to one another if we were to meet. It's not healthy to be completely in the dark and let one's imagination run riot. If I could really see her at last, perhaps I might be able to put the whole thing behind me."

"I don't think Alberto would be very pleased," he said.

"I know that," I admitted. "He wouldn't like it at all. He hates even to speak of her to me. He hates to think that we both exist and that one day we might even meet. He has to shuttle quite independently between us and live a double life. But I'm sick of thinking of things that it hurts him to have me think about. And I'm sick of not hurting him, too. I'm sick of being alone and in the dark, analysing my own thoughts."

Augusto puffed at his pipe and looked into the distance. The air was unusually clear, the wind blew in warmer gusts, and the clouds hovered over the mountaintops. Augusto's scarf blew fitfully now, and his serious, stolid face gave me a feeling of stability. We went back down the hill, and I looked back at the woman with the sheaf of wheat, raising her bronze breasts into the bright clear air. I would remember her, I said to myself, and think of this day if Augusto and I ever became lovers.

"I was in love with Giovanna myself years ago," he said. I didn't answer right away. It was as if I had always known something of the sort. "That was when I got the revolver," he added.

"What revolver?"

"Alberto and I each bought one. We were all for committing suicide. We decided to shoot ourselves, each one of us in his own room, at exactly the same minute. I stared all night long at that revolver lying on my table and couldn't screw up my courage to go through with it. In the morning I went with my heart in my boots to Alberto's. But lo and behold, he was just getting ready to come and find me! We looked at each other and burst out laughing! Ever since then we've kept our revolvers loaded in our desks. I look at mine every once in a while, but I haven't any wish to shoot myself. All that was years ago. There are times when you're fed up with everything, but then the days and years sweep you along with them and you acquire some understanding. You understand that there's some meaning to even the stupidest things, and you don't take them as hard as you did before."

I realized that he was speaking in this vein for my benefit and trying in his own way to console me. I was grateful, but there was nothing I could say.

"Yes, it was a long time ago," he repeated. "All night long I stared at that revolver. Giovanna was going with someone else then, an orchestra conductor, and I couldn't stand the thought of her being crazy about him. I wanted her to leave her husband and the other man, too, and come and live with me. Alberto was in love with her, too, and we wandered around the city like madmen, stopping to drink in every bar. What fools we were! Well, we didn't kill ourselves; we just went on raving together. Finally one day it dawned on me that the orchestra conductor had dropped out of the picture and Alberto was his successor. He didn't have the nerve to tell me himself and wrapped the whole thing in mystery the way he does with you now. But I was past caring. I decided it wasn't worth while losing my head over anybody, and I began to study and write a book about the Polish wars of secession. I thought Alberto wouldn't last long with her either, and instead they've gone on with it until today. When I saw Giovanna again we became good friends, and I stayed friends with Alberto too. We reminisce quite often about that day when we had an urge to commit suicide. We're the damnedest fools when we're young!"

When we got back to the centre of town I said good-bye to Augusto and went home. Gemma was away and I had to cook supper, so I put the meat and potatoes on the stove. I missed the baby and wished I could sing to her about *Le bon roi Dagobert*. I hummed the tune while I was setting the table. When Alberto came in I asked him when he intended to go away. He sat down at the table and propped the newspaper up in front of him without making any reply. Finally he said in a low squeaky voice:

"Are you so anxious to get rid of me?"

"No," I said, "take your time."

But after supper he went into the study and began to pack his belongings in a zinc case. He dusted his books one by one as he put them in and took down the bust of Napoleon and his fleet of miniature ships. I watched him from the door. At a certain point he felt bored and sat down to read. I swept the kitchen and then went to bed.

She came on a Sunday. Augusto phoned me in the morning to tell me she would come, and in the afternoon he took Alberto to his apartment to listen to some new Negro records. I combed my hair and powdered my face and sat down to wait. All of a sudden I heard the ring of the bell at the garden gate. I pressed the button and heard the click it made when it opened. My hands were covered with a cold sweat; I clenched my teeth and swallowed hard. Then Giovanna walked in and we sat down in the drawing room face to face.

I saw that she was embarrassed, and this simplified everything. There was a blush on her cheeks, which gradually faded away, leaving her skin pale and of a cold, flourlike consistency. "So this is Giovanna," I said to myself as we sized each other up. She was hatless and had on her mouton fur piece, which appeared old and worn now that I could see it from close by. She held her gloves in her hands and sat with her legs crossed in the armchair near the window. I had imagined her as a vulgar sort of woman with a great deal of makeup and a violent cut to her features and body. Of all the mental pictures I had made of her the definitive one was violent and garish. But in real life there was nothing vulgar about her. Only after several minutes did I see that she was actually beautiful. Her face was pale and cold and her full, unpainted lips were smiling silently. She had small, white teeth, blue eyes, and her long narrow head with the grey-streaked black hair pinned up on top of it was turned slightly to one side.

"Where's the baby?" she asked.

"She's not here," I answered. "She's with my mother in the country."

"Too bad," she said. "I'd like to see her."

"I asked you to come here," I said. "Perhaps you're thinking it was an odd thing to do.... As a matter of fact, I haven't anything in particular to say. I was curious to see you, that's all. It was a pointless sort of curiosity, when you come down to it." She listened quietly, with her legs crossed and her worn gloves between her long fingers. "I have no intention of hurling accusations in your face or of getting down on my knees and begging you for mercy. I don't hate you, at least not so far as I know. There's nothing to do about it, I realize that. Alberto's going away. Then you'll be able to meet more often without his telling me lies. He says he hates to lie, but I don't know whether he really means it. We don't get on well together, that's the truth. Perhaps it's not your fault. I've done all I could to make a go of it, but with no luck. It's been a mess."

"It's warm in here," she said, taking off her fur. She had on a green knitted dress with a red *G* embroidered over the left breast. The dress wasn't especially pretty, and she had large, heavy breasts, wide hips, and thin arms and legs. She looked around and remarked: "The house is just the same. I used to come here sometimes when Alberto's mother was alive."

"You came to call on the old lady?"

"Yes," she said, laughing, "I came to play draughts with her. She was very fond of me. But she was a terrible tyrant. It's a good thing she died, because she'd have made life miserable for you. You'd have had to play draughts all day long, and if you'd forgotten yourself and won a game she'd never have forgiven you!"

"It's been miserable enough without that," I said.

Then she asked me if I had a picture of the baby. I showed her one, and after she had laid it down she drew a picture out of her own handbag.

"This is my son," she said. And I looked at a boy with bright eyes and full lips, wearing a sailor suit. "He won't study," she said. "Boys are hard to handle. It's much better to have a girl. He won't do his Latin. But the teachers are too hard on them."

I made tea and we drank it with some biscuits that she said were very good. The muscles of my face were taut and I felt very tired and ready for her to go. I wanted to ask her about the orchestra conductor and how she had met Alberto and fallen in love with him. But all I said was:

"Do you love him very much?"

"Yes," she said. "Very much indeed." She put her cup down on the table and both of us stood up.

"It's been eleven years now," she said. "I couldn't give him up." All of a sudden tears came into her eyes. "No, I couldn't possibly do it. I've thought of it often enough. I've been unfaithful and lied to him and said the cruellest things. We've sworn to put an end to it, then we've begun all over again, and I may say that now I know how much I love him. I can't give him up. I'm sorry." She pulled out a handkerchief and dabbed at her eyes. Then she blew her nose and rubbed her face, shaking her head at the same time. "I've been unhappy; I was on poor terms with my husband from the start. I'd have left him long ago if it weren't for the boy. He's not a bad man and I suppose he loves me in his own way. But we haven't anything to say to each other and he thinks I'm silly and queer. For a long time I thought I really was as silly and queer as he said. I tried to live up to what he expected of me; I went out and gave little tea parties and chatted with all the ladies. Then I was bored to death and gave up trying. He was terribly angry at first and made dreadful scenes, but finally he got over it and we settled down to tolerating one another. That's the way it's been with me." She put on her fur and gloves and tied a net scarf around her neck. "If I'd married Alberto," she said, "I might have been a different woman. Stronger and braver and more energetic. And perhaps he would have been a different man. Don't think I like him the way he is now. I know his weaknesses very well, and sometimes I find him positively hateful. But if we two had married it wouldn't have been the same. We met too late. We're stupid and don't know what we really want when we're young. Life runs away with us before we know what it's all about."

She took my hands in hers and squeezed them. She had a sad, hesitant smile on her face; perhaps she was wondering whether or not we should kiss each other good-bye. I put my face close to her cold face and had the scent of it in my nostrils for a second while we kissed.

"Too bad I didn't see the baby," she said as we went down the stairs.

After she was gone I realized that there were other things I wanted to say to her. But I was relieved to be alone and feel the muscles of my face gradually relaxing. I lay down on the sofa with a cushion under my head. It was dark outside. I always missed the baby when evening came and wondered if my mother was tucking her in tightly so that she wouldn't toss the blankets off in her sleep. I went into the kitchen and lit the gas under a kettle of soup. Then I called the cat and threw him some scraps of cheese.

I had thought that after seeing Giovanna I should feel more peaceful, and as a matter of fact I did. An icy calm spread through me. Where before there were fantastic but silent images, now I saw a woman drinking a cup of tea and showing me a picture of her son. I felt neither hate nor pity. I felt nothing at all. Inside there was a great black hole that made me even lonelier than before. Now I realized that those silent images of Giovanna had somehow peopled my solitude and kept me company. I was alone now, and when my hand groped for the picture I had made of her it found only an empty black hole and withdrew with a withering chill upon it. The real Giovanna who had sat in the armchair near the window did not hate me, and I did not hate her; indeed, there was no relationship of any kind between us.

I wondered when Alberto was going away and wished it would be soon. But he couldn't seem to make up his mind. I watched the bookshelves gradually empty themselves as every day he packed a few more books away in the zinc case. When they were altogether empty, I thought to myself, he would go away. We hardly talked to each other at all. I made lunch and supper and ironed his shirts because Gemma was away. He polished his own shoes and sometimes he helped me clear the table. Every morning I made his bed while he stood by the window waiting for me to finish.

I didn't tell him about Giovanna's visit, nor did I know whether or not she had told him. A few days later I went to Maona to get the baby. I meant to tell my mother that Alberto and I were separating, but when I saw her I didn't say anything. She was slicing ham in the kitchen when I arrived, and the baby had a cold. I said she must have tossed off the blankets in her sleep, and at this both my mother and father took offence. I went back in the bus with the baby in my arms and Gemma weeping like a fountain beside me because she was leaving her family. While we were rolling among the hills and fields that bordered the highway I held the baby tight and tried to imagine the time when we would be alone together. My mother had pinned her hair up in two braids around her head, and her thin, bare face had a new alert but melancholy expression. I had a feeling that she knew what had happened. She sat on my knees, crumbling a biscuit in her fingers and putting an occasional piece in her mouth. She didn't talk yet, but she seemed to understand everything. When we reached home we met Alberto coming out of the gate. He took the baby in his arms and kissed her, but she only started to cry. He set her down on the ground, shrugged his shoulders, and went on his way.

I telephoned Francesca, and when she came to see me I asked her if she felt like taking that long-delayed trip to San Remo with the baby and me. I told her that probably Alberto would leave in the next few days and I didn't want to be around and see him go. She was very pleased and said we'd go to the Hotel Bellevue, where they served hot ice cream every Saturday night. I asked her what that was and she said it was vanilla ice cream with a hot chocolate sauce over it. She looked up the trains and made all the arrangements in no time at all.

When Alberto came home he found me packing my bags. This time it was my turn to be going somewhere without him and he looked on in glum silence. I told him that Gemma would stay to look after him and asked him for some money, which he gave me. We left early the next morning while he was still asleep.

San Remo was very windy. At first we were all in one room, but Francesca couldn't stand the baby's crying and took another room for herself. For some days she hung about us and said that San Remo was a resort for doddering old gentlemen and she was bored to death with it.

Then she made friends with some people at the hotel and went out boating and dancing with them. She had any number of evening dresses, each one more beautiful than the next. I stayed with the baby until she fell asleep, and then I went downstairs with my knitting, but I was always afraid that the baby might wake up and cry, so I went to bed very early. When Francesca came up she knocked at my door and I went into her room and heard who had danced with her and what they had to say.

After we had been there a fortnight Augusto came to join us. He was ill-humoured and jealous, and Francesca treated him very shabbily. He sat smoking in the hotel lobby and wrote a chapter of his new book on the origins of Christianity. I asked him if Alberto were at the house and he said that he was still slowly packing his books in the zinc case. I wanted to talk to him about Giovanna, but he cut me short because he was in too gloomy a mood to listen. Sometimes he walked silently up and down the pavement with the baby and me, looking around for Francesca's plaid coat. Francesca didn't want him about. She had made friends with a countess, and every night she got drunk with her and they went to the casino. She was bored with all her evening dresses and made herself a new one out of a long black skirt and some silk scarves sewed together. She painted a picture of the countess stretched out on a tiger skin and she was always telling me that the countess's children weren't little pests like mine.

The baby had begun to talk. Every day she said something new and I thought she was very clever. When she had eaten her biscuit she stretched out both hands and said: "More!" with a wily, melancholy smile. Every morning she stood up in her bed and said: "Baby sleep no more!" and I would take her and the camel into my bed and make the camel walk up and down on the bedcover. Then Francesca would come in wearing a wrapper, with cold cream on her face and her hair in curlers, smoke a cigarette, and tell me between yawns about the evening she had spent with the countess.

I told her she ought to be a little nicer to Augusto. She was heartless, I told her, to lead him a life like this. Every now and then they went for a walk together, and perhaps they found a place to make love somewhere because he always seemed slightly more cheerful when they returned. But then the countess and her friends whistled under Francesca's window and she powdered her face in a hurry, threw on her plaid coat, and ran to join them. I never knew whether she had taken a liking to one of the men in the party or not. She said no. She said that they were amusing, while Augusto was solemn and jealous and his origins of Christianity bored her to death.

The baby was taken ill on November seventeenth. She was upset all day long and would not eat. It was Saturday and they served the famous hot ice cream, but she cried and spat it all over the place, until I lost patience and struck her across the hands. She cried and cried, and I didn't know what to do. She didn't want to hear about *Le bon roi Dagobert* or have her camel beside her or anything. She cried steadily until ten o'clock in the evening, and then she fell asleep. I lowered her gently into the bed and sat down beside her. She slept for half an hour or so, but very lightly, shifting about and twitching at intervals. Francesca dropped in to see me on her way to a dance at the casino. She had combed her hair back from her forehead in a strange new way and painted her lips a colour that was almost yellow. She had on what she called her Hindu dress, the one made of silk scarves sewed together, and a wide silver lamé sash around her waist. The effect was really stunning. She looked down at the baby and said she must have worms to twitch that way in her sleep. She walked around the room, and I hated her for making so much noise. Then the countess whistled under the window and off she went.

While she was running down the hall the baby woke up screaming and I picked her up in my arms. She seemed burning hot, and so I took her temperature. The thermometer read

102. I paced up and down the room with her, wondering what could be the matter. She was breathing hard and twisting her lips. It couldn't be just an ordinary fever. She had been feverish a number of times, but never before had she cried so desperately. I tried asking her what hurt, but she only cried louder and pushed away my hands. I was terrified. Finally I laid her down on the bed and went to call Augusto. He was lying fully dressed on his bed with the light on, and there was a distressed look in his half-closed eyes because Francesca had gone to the dance without him. I told him that the baby was very sick and asked him to go and get a doctor. He sat up and smoothed his hair without really understanding what I had said. Then he pulled himself together and put on his overcoat. I went back to my room, picked up the baby, and paced up and down, holding her wrapped in a blanket. She had a red face and excessively bright eyes. Every now and then she fell asleep, only to wake up again with a start. I thought of how men and women spend their time tormenting one another and how stupid it all seems when you are face to face with something like a baby's fever. I remembered how once upon a time I had tormented myself waiting tremblingly for Alberto and wondered how I could have attached importance to anything so idiotic. I was badly frightened, but beneath my fright there was a feeling that the baby was going to get well and Francesca would tease me for being such an alarmist. So many times before I had been scared to death over nothing at all.

Then Augusto came back with the doctor, a red-haired young man with a freckled face. I hurriedly and nervously undressed the baby on the bed. She was crying more feebly now as the doctor held her thin little body in his hands and Augusto looked on in silence. The doctor said that he couldn't diagnose her trouble, but he saw no reason for concern. He prescribed a mild sedative and Augusto went to have it made up at a pharmacy. Then the doctor went away, saying he would come back in the morning. Augusto stayed with me and I felt much calmer. The baby went to sleep and I looked at her thin, red face and perspiration-drenched hair. I asked Augusto not to go away because I was still frightened to be alone.

At three o'clock in the morning the baby screamed. She grew purple in the face and threw up the small portion of ice cream I had forced down her the evening before. She waved her arms and legs and pushed me away. The chambermaid and a woman who had the room next to mine came in and suggested I give her an enema prepared with camomile. While I was preparing it Francesca appeared at the door, looking very drunk. Hating her with all my might, I shouted:

"Go away!"

She went into her room and came back a few minutes later, after she had apparently bathed her face in cold water. She asked the maid to get her a cup of strong coffee. I hated her so much that I couldn't look her in the face. My throat was dry and constricted with terror. The baby was not crying any more; she lay there under the blanket with all the colour gone out of her cheeks, breathing jerkily.

"You nincompoops!" said Francesca. "Can't you see she's in a very bad way? You've got to get a doctor."

The maid told her that one had already come, but Francesca said none of the San Remo doctors was any good except the countess's doctor. She spoke in a loud voice and a decisive manner, as if to show that she was no longer drunk. She went out to look for the countess's doctor, and Augusto went with her, leaving me alone with the woman who had suggested the enema. Her face was heavy and wrinkled, with powder caked in the furrows; she wore a violet kimono and spoke with a strong German accent. For some reason her presence was very reassuring; I had complete confidence in her heavy, wrinkled face. She told me that the baby must have an upset stomach and such a disturbance often takes on terrifying forms. Her son had had an attack of the same kind when he was a baby. And now he was a grown man—she raised her hand to show me how tall he was—who had taken a degree in engineering and got himself engaged to be married.

It was growing light outside. The sun rose out of a greenish haze and shone upon the sea. On the terrace in front of the hotel a waiter in a white jacket was setting wicker chairs and tables in order among the palms, and another man in a striped outfit was dipping a mop into a bucket of water. Now the sun was red and glaring. I hated the sea and the wicker furniture and the palm trees. Why had I come to San Remo anyhow? What was I doing in this room with the woman in a violet kimono? I hated Francesca and thought to myself that she and Augusto must have stopped at the countess's for drinks and have had one too many.

They did come back, though, with the countess's doctor, a tall, bald man with a thin, ivory face and a pendulous lower lip, disclosing teeth that were long and yellow like those of a horse. He said that neither the sedative nor the enema was any use. Everything that had been done so far was wrong. He wrote out another prescription, and while Augusto went back to the pharmacy he questioned me about the baby's health in recent months and how she had been taken ill. While I was telling him he held the camel in his hand and made it walk up and down the rug. Somehow his gesture gave me hope. I asked him if it was something serious and he said he didn't think so but he couldn't yet say for sure. He could advance various hypotheses, but none of them was definitive. He sent away the woman in the kimono because he said there should be as few people as possible in a sickroom in order to conserve the supply of oxygen. Francesca brought me a cup of coffee. It was a bright, sunny day, and the usual old gentlemen were sitting on the terrace, holding their canes between their knees and reading their newspapers.

At nine o'clock, just as the bald doctor was cleaning a syringe in order to make an injection, the freckle-faced doctor of the previous evening came back. He seemed a little offended, but Francesca took him out in the hall and talked to him in private. Then the two doctors held a consultation together. The baby was quiet now and breathing evenly. She seemed very tired, with white lips and dark circles around her eyes. She stood up on the bed and said:

"Sleep no more!"

These were the first words she had spoken since she had fallen ill, and I was so happy that I burst into tears. Francesca held me in her arms.

"I thought she was going to die," I murmured. Francesca patted my shoulders without speaking. "I thought she was going to die for certain. I thought so all night long. I was scared to death." I wanted to make up to Francesca somehow for the hate I had felt for her at three o'clock in the morning. "You looked very handsome in your Hindu dress. And the way you had your hair fixed was very becoming."

"Don't you think we ought to send a wire to Alberto?" she said. "She's the poor devil's daughter, after all."

"Yes," I said. "But isn't she better?"

"Perhaps so," she said. "But I'd send him a wire just the same."

At eleven o'clock the baby began to scream again, shaking and twitching all over, with a fever of 103. In the afternoon she fell asleep but only for a few minutes. Augusto went to send the wire. I began to wish Alberto would arrive immediately. I paced up and down the room, holding the baby wrapped in a blanket. Francesca stepped out in the hall every now and then for a cigarette. The doctor went out to dinner and came back. I could read no hope in his gloomy, disdainful face with the pendulous lower lip. Everyone looked as if there were no hope, and I wanted to tell them that I knew she was better. She looked better to me, and for a moment, when she was in Francesca's arms, she began to play with her necklace.

> Le bon roi Dagobert
> Chassait dans la plaine de l'Enfer!

Men and women strolled along the pavement or sat comfortably in the wicker chairs among the palm trees. They smoked cigarettes, flicked the ashes away, tucked plaid blankets around their legs, and showed each other cartoons in the papers. A boy came by selling fresh oranges, and they pressed them in their fingers and counted the change in the palms of their hands.

> Le bon roi Dagobert
> A mis sa culotte à l'envers!

I remembered with horror how I had struck the baby across the hands when she would not eat her supper and how she had thrown down her spoon and started to cry disconsolately. I looked into her big brown eyes and thought that she knew all there was to know about me. Her eyes were weary and dull, and their lack of expression was dreadful on a baby's face. She had a faraway, bitter look, unreproaching but at the same time pitiless, as if she had nothing more to ask. I stopped rocking her in my arms and laid her down on the bed under a shawl. She sobbed convulsively and pushed away my hands.

Suddenly Francesca began to cry and went out of the room. I looked at the doctor and he looked at me. His damp, red, pendulous lower lip gave him the appearance of an animal drinking. The freckled doctor came back with another, smaller doctor who seemed to be someone very important. I asked them if I should undress the baby and they said no. The little doctor felt her neck and forehead and tapped her knees with an ivory stick. Then they went away. I was left alone with the bald doctor, and all of a sudden his pendulous lower lip reminded me of something indecent, like the sexual parts of a dog. Then he told me it might be meningitis. At ten o'clock in the evening the baby died.

Francesca took me into her room and I lay down on her bed and drank a cup of coffee. The woman in the violet kimono and the manager of the hotel and the freckle-faced doctor all came to see me. The woman told me I'd have other children. She said that when children die young it isn't so bad. It's worse when they're older. She had lost a son who was a lieutenant in the Navy, and she raised her hand to show me how tall he was. But the hotel manager said it was harder to lose children when they were small. Finally Francesca sent them all away and told me to go to sleep.

I shut my eyes, but there was one sight I couldn't get away from. It was the expression in the baby's face when I was rocking her in my arms. Her eyes were bitter and indifferent, indifferent even to *Le bon roi Dagobert*. I could see all her clothes and toys: the camel, the ball, the squeaking rubber cat, the leggings, the galoshes, and the apron with Snow White and the

Seven Dwarfs on it. I remembered the things she ate and the words she knew how to say. Then I fell asleep and dreamed I was walking along a road and bumped up against a stone wall, which made me wake up screaming.

I called Francesca, but she wasn't in the room. There was only Augusto, standing by the window with his head against the glass. He said Francesca had gone in to the baby and asked me if there was anything I wanted. I asked him to sit down beside me, and he sat there, holding my hand and stroking my hair. Then I began to cry. I cried all night long, with my face buried in the pillow. I hung on to his hand and said things that made no sense. As long as I cried or talked I could forget about the camel and the ball. Alberto arrived at five o'clock in the morning. He dropped his bag and ran sobbing to kneel down beside me, and his head of curly grey hair on my shoulder seemed to be the only thing in the world I needed.

I told Alberto that I never wanted to see the camel or the ball again, and Francesca and he made a bundle of all the baby's things and gave them away. Francesca left San Remo several days before us and removed from the house the baby's carriage, crib, and all the rest of her belongings. At the same time she told Gemma to go and pay a visit to her family at Maona. Gemma left in tears, taking the cat with her. I couldn't bear to see her because I should have been reminded of the stye in her eye when she bent over me the day the baby was born. Alberto wrote to my mother and father that I didn't want to see them but preferred to be alone with him for a while. I didn't want anyone else, and they must be patient and let me fill my own needs as I thought best. Everyone reacts to sorrow in his own particular way, he told them, and throws up the best defences he can. And in such cases the family and friends must hold their peace and stand by quietly until it is over.

We went back to the city, and for a while I didn't leave the house because I didn't want to see any children. At first a woman came to do the cleaning, but it was so hard for me to talk to her that finally I told her not to come and did the work myself. Still I didn't have very much to do. I stayed in bed late in the morning, watching my arms lie empty and free on the bedcover. Then I slowly got dressed and let the empty hours of the day drag by. I tried not to think of the song about *Le bon roi Dagobert,* but it rang continually in my ears. And I still saw in front of me the doctor's mouth, like that of an animal drinking, the long halls and red-carpeted stairways of the Hotel Bellevue and the wicker chairs and palm trees on the terrace below.

Alberto stayed at home a great deal. He was extremely kind, and I was amazed by his efforts to help me. We never mentioned the baby, and I noticed that he had taken away the oatmeal and the rest of her food that Francesca had forgotten. He read Rilke's poems out loud and also some of the notes he had written on the margins of various books. He said that some day or other he wanted to put all these notes together in a volume which he would call *Variations on a Minor Scale.* I think he was slightly envious of Augusto for the books he had published. Anyhow, he said I was to help put the notes in order, and sometimes he had me work over them on the typewriter until late at night. I didn't type fast enough to keep up with his dictation, but he never lost his temper. He even told me that I should make comments on anything that didn't seem clear to me.

One day I asked him if he was going away and he said no. Sooner or later, he said, he'd empty the zinc case where he'd begun to pack his books. Meanwhile it sat there in his study, half filled with his things. When he wanted one particular book he had quite a time digging it out, but still he didn't get around to putting everything back on the shelves. We spent most of the time in the study, and he never said a word about wanting to go out. At first we didn't talk about the baby, but later we did, and he said perhaps it was good for me to unburden myself to him. He said that we'd have another child and that even if now this prospect gave me no pleasure, I would love the new one just as well, and all my peace of mind would come back to me when I saw it lying at my side. We made love together and gradually I began to imagine the time when I would have another baby. I thought of how I would nurse it and rock it, and of all my thoughts this was the only one from which I got any satisfaction.

Then I began to fall in love again with Alberto, and the realization of it frightened me. I trembled now at the idea of his going away, and the sight of the zinc case became painful. When I typed to his dictation I was afraid of going too slowly, and when he looked at me I imagined that he didn't like my face. I reflected how easy everything was for other women—Francesca and Giovanna, for instance, who never seemed to have known even the shadow of my great fear. How easy life is, I thought, for women who are not afraid of a man. I stared for a long time at my face in the mirror. It had never been very pretty, and now it seemed to me that every trace of youth and freshness was gone.

Alberto and I were always at home, and I understood now how a man and woman live together. He never went out, and I saw him from one end of the day to the other. I saw him get up in the morning and drink the cup of coffee I had made for him;

I saw him bend over and dig into the zinc case and make notes on the margins of his books. We made love on his couch in the study and lay awake in the darkness while I felt him breathing calmly beside me. Before going to sleep he always told me to wake him up if I felt sad. I didn't dare actually wake him, but the thought that I could if I wanted to was a great consolation. He was so very kind that now I knew what a man's tenderness could be. It was my own fault, I realized, if even now I wasn't altogether happy with him. I was always worried about my face and body, and when we made love I was afraid he might be bored. Every time I had something to say to him I thought it over to make sure it wasn't boring. When he read me the notes he wanted to make into a book occasional comments came into my mind. But when one day I finally said something he seemed displeased and explained to me at length why I was wrong. I could have bitten off my tongue for having spoken. I remembered the time before we were married when we sat endlessly in cafés and I babbled on without stopping. Then it was easy enough for me to talk. I said whatever came into my head and moved before him with all the confidence of youth. Now that I had had the baby and the baby was dead I couldn't bear the idea of his leaving me.

"Why *don't* you go away?" I said. "I know it's just that you're sorry for me. Why don't you go?"

"I don't like the idea of your being here alone," he replied.

"I never expected you to be so kind," I went on. "I didn't dream you'd try to help me as much as you've done. I didn't think you cared much for the baby or for me either. I thought you cared only for Giovanna."

He chuckled quietly, as if to himself. "Sometimes I think I don't care for anyone," he said.

"Not even for Giovanna?"

"No, not even for Giovanna," he said. "She and her husband have gone to their country house near the lakes, and I don't know when she'll be back. When I don't see her I hardly ever think of her at all. Queer, isn't it?"

We were silent for a few minutes. He lay at my side breathing quietly, toying with my hand on the bedcover. He opened my fingers and closed them suddenly; he tickled my palm, then put my hand down and drew away.

"It's difficult to know what we have inside of us. We're here today and gone today. I've never understood myself properly. I was very fond of my mother, for instance, and terribly sad to see her go. Then one morning I walked out of the house with a cigarette in my mouth, and just as I was striking a match to light it I had a sudden feeling of relief. I was almost glad that she was dead, that I would never have to play draughts with her again or hear her irritated tone of voice when I put too much sugar in her coffee. That's how it is that I don't really know how much I care for Giovanna. I haven't seen her for several months now, and I can't say I've thought very much about her. I'm lazy, when you come down to it, and I don't want to suffer."

"And when she comes back," I said, "do you think you'll want to go away?"

"I don't know," he answered. "I might, at that."

As I lay awake I remembered that he had told me to call him whenever I felt too sad. But I didn't have the nerve to do it, and besides I was beginning to realize that there was no use counting on him for anything. It was absurd to expect anything from a man like Alberto. Even Giovanna couldn't really count on him. I looked at his sleeping face, with the immobile lips that gave no answer. Would he stay or go? Did he really want to have another child? I lay there with my eyes wide open and said to myself: "I'll never know what he really wants. I'll never know."

It was then that I remembered the revolver. I began to think about it in somewhat the same way as I had thought of nursing another baby. The idea of it calmed me and I thought of it while I was making the bed or peeling potatoes or ironing Alberto's shirts or going up and down the stairs. If I were to have another baby I'd be in constant fear that it might take ill and die. I was tired of being afraid, and now that I understood him there didn't seem to be much point to bearing a child for Alberto.

Francesca came occasionally to see me, and she told me that she had a new lover. He was a man she had met with the countess at San Remo, and she had given up painting in order to spend all of her time with him. She said she had a weakness for him, but nothing too serious, and that he was somewhat of a gangster, so that I shouldn't be surprised if I read in the paper one day that he had strangled her in her sleep. He was strictly no good, she said, and every time he left her she went to make sure he hadn't broken into her jewellery. But he was a handsome devil, and she liked to be seen with him, because women all turned their heads to stare, and for quite some time he had been a fancy man to the countess. She said that the countess was an old bitch and a dreadful miser because she wouldn't buy the picture she had painted of her. When the countess had come back from San Remo they had had a terrible row over Francesca's new lover. Francesca didn't want to hear any more of Augusto, and Augusto didn't want to hear of her either. But Augusto came to see us very seldom because he was working hard to finish his book on the origins of Christianity.

Alberto read his notes to him and tried to interest him in his writing, but Augusto hardly paid any attention. He seemed to prefer being with me and often he hung about watching me iron shirts. I thought of the windy day when we had gone for a walk together and I had imagined making love with him. When I looked at his face I felt that he was a little like me, with his eyes continually staring into a well of darkness within him. For this reason I thought that we might be happy as lovers and that he might understand and help me. But then I told myself that it was too late, too late to start something new like falling in love or having another baby. It was too hard work, and I was tired. Looking at Augusto, I remembered the night at San Remo when the baby was taken ill and the night after, when I had lain clutching his hand. There are other things in life, I told myself, than making love or having children. There are a thousand things to do, and one of them is writing a book on the origins of Christianity. My own life seemed to me meagre and limited, but it was too late to change it, and back of all my thoughts now there was always the image of the revolver.

Alberto had begun to go out again. He said that he was going to the office, but I was sure that Giovanna must be back. He said that she wasn't, but I didn't believe him. Then one day Giovanna came to see me. It was in the morning, and Alberto had gone out, leaving me to type his notes.

This time Giovanna was dressed in grey with a round, straw hat and a sort of cape over her shoulders. Her hat and dress were new, but she was wearing the same worn gloves as she had worn before. She sat down and started immediately to speak of the baby. She said that she had written me a letter and then torn it up because it seemed silly to send it. I had been very much in her thoughts, she said, but she hesitated a long time before coming to see me, until finally she had put on her hat and come. I looked at her hat, and it didn't seem to me like a hat that had been put on in a hurry. It was a stiff little hat, and I wondered if it didn't press against her forehead. She spoke quietly and simply, as if she were trying not to give me pain. But I didn't want to talk to her about the baby.

"It's very odd," she said, "but I dreamed about your baby for two or three nights in succession just before she died. I dreamed that we were in this drawing room, and Alberto's mother was here, too, lying on the couch, wrapped in a blanket. She said that she felt cold and I threw my fur over her and she thanked me for it. The baby was sitting on a little stool, and she was afraid the baby might get a chill and asked me to shut the window. I had bought the baby a doll and I wanted to take it out of the package, but I couldn't seem to untie the string."

"The baby didn't play with dolls," I said. "She played with a ball and a camel."

"I thought the dream was a strange one," she went on. "I woke up in a state of anxiety, which I couldn't explain. Then a few days later I got a letter from Alberto about the baby."

I looked at her hard and tried to make out whether she had really had any such dream. I had a strong suspicion that she was making the whole thing up.

"He wrote only a very few words," she said. "We had guests that day and I had to talk to them and entertain them. And all the time I was in distress. Strange to say, I wasn't thinking of Alberto as much as I was of you."

She sat in an armchair with her slender legs crossed, her hands folded underneath her cape, and her hat perched stiffly on her head.

"That hat must hurt you," I said.

"Yes, it does," she answered, pulling it off and revealing a red mark on her forehead.

I looked at her hard. She had a kind and peaceful expression on her face, and her body was peaceful and cool in her new spring dress. I imagined her picking it out of a fashion journal and ordering a dressmaker to make it. I thought of the succession of peaceful days that made up her existence and of her body that knew neither uncertainty nor fear.

"Do you hate me?" she asked.

"No," I said. "I don't exactly hate you. But I don't want to talk to you. I don't see any point to our being in the same room. I think it's stupid and ridiculous. Because we'll never speak of really important things or be honest with one another. I don't really believe you had that dream, you know. I believe you made it up on your way here."

"No," she said, and began to laugh. "I can't make things up. Hasn't Alberto told you that I have no imagination?"

"No. We don't talk much about you. Once when we did talk about you he said that he didn't think of you often when you were away. That should have made me feel better, but it only made me feel worse. It means that he doesn't love anyone, not even you. Nothing is sacred to him. Once upon a time I was jealous and hated you, but now all that's gone. Don't think for a minute that he's unhappy without you. He refuses to be unhappy. He just lights a cigarette and walks away."

"I know," she said. "You can't tell me anything about him that I don't know. You forget how long I've known him. Time has gone by and now we're no longer young. We've grown old together, he in his house and I in mine, but together just the same. We've said good-bye over and over, but we've always come together again. He didn't make the first move, that's true. I did. But he was always very glad. We get on well together. You can't understand him because you started off on the wrong foot."

"Please go away," I said. "If you stay any longer I shall begin to hate you."

"Hate me, if you like," she said. "You're quite within your rights. Perhaps I hate you too. But I'm sorry your baby died. I have a child myself and I feel sorry for any woman who loses one. After I had read Alberto's letter I couldn't think of anything else all day. I was stunned."

"I don't want Alberto to write you," I said. "I don't want you to meet and take walks and trips together and talk about the baby and me. After all, he's my husband. Perhaps I shouldn't have married him in the first place, but I did, and we had a child and lost her. This can't be wiped out just because you two enjoy making love together."

"Perhaps what's passed between Alberto and me can't be wiped out either," she murmured as if to herself. She put on her hat, frowning, and slowly pulled on her gloves, looking at every finger.

"I don't know what there's been between you two," I said. "Important things, no doubt, but not as important as the birth and death of a baby. Little trips you've had, haven't you? And little walks together. But go away now, will you? I'm tired of seeing you there in front of me. I'm tired of your dress and hat. I'm saying things that don't make sense. If you stay here any longer I may want to kill you."

"No, you won't," she said with a shrill, youthful laugh. "You wouldn't do a thing like that. You look like too much of a simple country girl. And I'm not the least bit afraid of you."

"So much the better," I said, "but go away."

"Very well, I'm going," she said. "But I shall remember this day. It's a landmark, somehow. I don't know exactly why. But I have a feeling that we've said a lot of honest and important things to each other. I'll come to see you again, if you don't mind."

"I'd rather not, thank you just the same," I said.

"Well, you say what you mean, anyhow, don't you?" she said. "Don't hate me too much." And she went away.

I went back to my typing, but I couldn't keep my mind on it and made any number of mistakes. I went over to the mirror to see if I really looked like a simple country girl. By the time lunch was ready Alberto had come home. I asked him if I looked like a simple country girl, and he looked at me hard for a minute before he said no. Then he added that he didn't know what a simple country girl would look like anyhow. He was nervous and distracted and immediately after lunch he went out again.

I wanted to phone Francesca or go and see her, but I remembered that she was probably with her new lover. Alberto went back to going out every day and sometimes in the evening as well. Now that I was sleeping in the study he no longer locked the door, so very often when I was alone in the evening I opened the desk drawer and looked at the revolver. To look at it like that calmed me down, and afterwards I shut the drawer very slowly and went to bed. I lay awake in the darkness, trying not to remember the time when the baby's feeble and plaintive cry used to break the silence of the night. My thoughts carried me far away to the time when I was a child in Maona. I remembered a certain black cream that my mother used to put on my hands to cure me of chilblains, and I could see the face of an old school teacher with glasses who used to take us on picnics, and that of a monk who came every Sunday to ask charity of my mother and carried with him a grey sack full of dry crusts of bread. I thought of how I used to read *From Slavegirl to Queen* and how I had hidden in the coal cellar and wept one day when my mother had made me a pale blue dress to wear to a school party and I had thought it was very pretty and then discovered it wasn't pretty at all. I realized that I was saying good-bye to all these things, as if I were about to take leave of them forever, and, closing my eyes, I could smell the black cream on my hands and the odour of the baked pears that my mother used to feed us in cold weather.

When Alberto came home on nights like these we would make love together. But he no longer spoke of our having any more children. He was bored with dictating notes for his book and he glanced constantly at his watch all the time that he was in the house. Sometimes it occurred to me that soon he would be too old and tired to go out and then he would sit in an armchair and dictate to me and ask me to take his things out of the zinc case, to put the books back on the shelves and the miniature ships in their accustomed place. But Alberto was just the same as ever, older and yet incorrigibly young. He walked at a brisk pace and stuck his thin head forward as if to drink in the air of the street, with his open raincoat flapping across his slight body and a lighted cigarette between his lips. Between the eyes I shot him.

He had asked me to put some tea in a thermos bottle to take with him on his trip. He had always said that I was good at making tea. I wasn't especially good at ironing or cooking, but my tea was the best he had ever tasted. He was slightly annoyed when it came to packing his bag because his shirts weren't very well ironed, particularly between the sleeves and the collar. He packed his bag alone, saying he didn't want me to help him. He put in on top several books from the zinc case. I suggested the poems of Rilke, but he turned them down.

"I know them by heart," he said.

I put some books in my bag too. When he saw me packing he was glad and said it would do me good to go to Maona and have my mother bring me my coffee in bed in the morning. I asked him what he was going to do about the zinc case.

"The zinc case?" he said, and started to laugh. "I'm not going away for good, you know. Did you think I was? Is that why you have such a solemn face?"

I went to look in the mirror and said:

"A very ordinary sort of face. The face of a simple country girl."

"Yes, a simple country girl," he said, and stroked my hair. Then he asked me to make him the tea, which he liked strong and very sweet.

"Tell me the truth, Alberto," I said.

"What truth?" he echoed.

"You're going away together."

"Who are going away together?" And then he added jokingly:

> She seeketh Truth, which is so dear
> As knoweth he who life for her refuses.

When I came back to the study he had completed the sketch. He showed it to me and laughed. It was a long, long train with a big cloud of black smoke swirling over it. He wet the tip of the pencil with his tongue in order to make the smoke thicker. I put the thermos bottle down on the desk. He was laughing and turned around to see if I was laughing too.

I shot him between the eyes.

My feet were wet and cold and my blistered heel hurt me at every step. The streets were quite empty and they glistened in the

gentle rain. I wanted to go to Francesca's, but I thought probably she was with her lover. And so I went home. There was
a dead silence, which I tried my very best not to hear. When
I reached the kitchen I knew what I was going to do. It was
very easy and I was not afraid. I knew now that I would never
have to talk to the man with the olive complexion sitting behind the desk in the police station, and this genuinely relieved
me. I would never talk to anyone again. Not to Francesca or
Giovanna or Augusto or my mother. To no one. I sat down at
the marble-top table, where I could not escape listening to the
silence. A cold, rank smell came up out of the sink, and the
alarm clock ticked on the shelf. I took pen and ink and began
to write in the notebook where I kept an account of household
expenses. All of a sudden I asked myself for whose benefit I
was writing. Not for Giovanna or Francesca, not even for my
mother. For whom, then? It was too difficult to decide, and I felt
that the time of conventional and clear-cut answers had come
forever to a stop within me.